A TALE FROM
WEST SIDE
WILMINGTON

JUAN DIAZ

STRATTON
—PRESS—
Publishing Life

A TALE FROM WEST SIDE WILMINGTON
Copyright © 2021 **Juan Diaz**

Stratton Press Publishing
831 N Tatnall Street Suite M #188,
Wilmington, DE 19801
www.stratton-press.com
1-888-323-7009

ISBN (Paperback): 978-1-64895-332-3
ISBN (Ebook): 978-1-64895-333-0

Printed in the United States of America

Part One

Sammy

CHAPTER ONE

"**Y**ou being released today, Sammy?" The sound of my cell mate's question bounced off the concrete walls of our jail cell, seeming to ride the wave of optimism that encompassed the atmosphere around us. He knew the answer to that question, but he just liked to hear it spoken because it gave him some form of hope to latch on to.

"Yup, at 9:45 this very morning will be the last time my old Puerto Rican ass will see these walls." The words came out of my mouth with renewed optimism, as if being rinsed off by the cleansing release of a giggle.

I stood in the middle of my cell buttoning up the cuff of the left sleeve of my light blue dress shirt, trying to hold back the emotions that threatened to break free from the calm facade that I was displaying to my cell mate. Shit, I know I had every right to be at least a little emotional at that moment. I had been locked up in this bitch they call Stone Gate Prison since 1995 on some murder rap, but thanks to some strings that lawyer pulled, I got the charges lowered, allowing me to serve twenty-two years of what was once a life sentence. I don't know how he did it, but my lawyer, Donald Goldman, was a fucking genius. Well, I wouldn't expect anything less from a lawyer who got reputed Italian mobsters and killers off the sights of the RICO Act.

So yeah, I had every right to shed a tear of happiness, but I wasn't going to do it in front of my cell mate. I was the guy's hero, for God's sake. I didn't want to look like a pussy in front of him.

"Yo, Reggie, how I look, man?" I said, turning toward my cell mate, who was laid up on the bottom bunk with his hands supporting the back of his head in a nonchalant, relaxed pose, looking like a man who didn't have a care in the world.

Reggie turned his head slowly toward the direction I was standing without removing his hands from the back of his head and started, "Man, you look like one of those white boys that are fresh out of college seeking to get a job at one of those social media startups. Shit, with those tight-ass khaki pants and that light blue dress shirt you have on, who knows what you might do." Reggie said this in between giggles that carried with them the essence of a friendly nature, inviting me to keep the joke going.

"Fucking *maricon*," I said as I waved my hand toward him in a "forget you" gesture, which prompted Reggie into a fit of laughter. His thick baritone laughter filling up our cell somehow seemed to illuminate it, chasing away the dark and drab that were always housed within it.

"Dude, all jokes aside, I wish you the best of luck out there, you hear."

I stood there and listened to him, as Reggie mustered every ounce of seriousness into his words. "I know what I just said to you came off a bit cliché, but you were given a second chance at life, which doesn't come too often for many." Reggie was now sitting on the edge of the bottom bunk with his bare feet firmly planted on the concrete floor. Before continuing to speak, Reggie reached under his bunk without breaking from his sitting position, except for his arm, which dragged out an extra-large Save-A-Lot grocery bag that gleamed in the faint florescent lights throughout the corridor of their cell block.

I already knew what was in the bag, of course. In that grocery bag was my future, the one ticket that would redeem me from my life of crime and establish me as a fully rehabilitated member of society. Within that bag were thirty yellow legal pads worth of my story. The blue lines of every sheet in that legal pad were the veins that my story coursed through, giving birth to an entire new perspective for my life. Yeah, I had written my autobiography and kept it in that damn shopping bag for seventeen years, and upon my release from this hellhole of a prison, I would try to get it published.

Reggie continued to speak, but this time his voice raised an octave as it began filling with emotion. "I read your whole book last week, man. Let's just say, my nigga, that shit was phenomenal," he stated, his voice quivering emotion as he now held the bag on his lap. He got up from the bed and walked toward me, holding out the bag gently in his hands as though he held a precious gift sent down from the heavens. "Now you take this manuscript and make sure that it is sent to the right people, you hear me. And don't put this masterpiece in the hands of a vanity press either. Shit, as good as that manuscript is, everyone in the world should be lining up to pay you for your book." Finishing off his last words, Reggie handed me the bag and opened up his track-riddled arms to embrace me. Those arms were a sheer reminder of Reggie's hard-won battle with heroin addiction. "I love you, brother, remember that. Thanks for everything you've done for me while you were in here with me."

Hearing that kind of gratitude pour so freely from the man's heart, the memory of the first time that I met him was triggered, as if someone turned on an old film projector on the theater of my mind. On its big screen, I could see a young and strung-out Reggie, whose golden-brown skin was ashy and riddled with open scabs so fresh some of them were a bright crimson. "Hey, man, you got a cigarette?" Reggie asked as he sat down on the bottom bunk, which, as far as he was concerned, was his spot for as long as he resided in prison.

"Nah, I don't smoke, man," I said to him, trying not to feel sorry him and failing miserably. Although he was young, I couldn't help but notice that the guy reminded me of my old man. He too was a big-time heroin addict.

Immediately, I recalled the day that Reggie first came to prison. He arrived in a line of newbies back in 2012. It was easy to tell that he was a heroin addict by the way he jittered and shivered his way along with the other newbies, not to mention that he was incessantly scratching his arms, where there were open track wounds that seemed to resemble the mouths of tortured souls screaming out in agony. The corrections officers that were there that day assigned me to get acclimated to the prison routine, which would spark one of the deepest friendships I ever had with any man in my life. Many nights I would hold Reggie in my as he whimpered in pain as symptoms of heroin withdrawal ravaged his body, like a man possessed by demons. It was during those bouts of withdrawal that I took the time to tell him about my life as a hit man working for the Puerto Rican crime family known as the Zepedas, but the streets called them *Los Cucos* (Spanish for *The Boogiemen*). Man, the shit I told Reggie could have landed me on death row, but I knew deep in my heart that Reggie wasn't a snitch. Plus, he knew damn well that if he snitched anything to the COs, there would be at least twenty prisoners on *Los Cucos'* payroll that would snuff him out, no questions asked.

"Yo, thank you so much for seeing me through my withdrawals," said Reggie, breaking me out of my reveries and bringing me back to the present. "Dude, you've been a great friend to me, hell, probably the only friend that I ever had in my whole entire life," he said dramatically, tightening his hug.

"All right, all right, faggots, break it up," said a white CO sarcastically. "That's just what this world needs, a spic and a nigger trying to make babies. News flash, shitheads, just cause Bruce Jenner gone up and turned hisself into a woman doesn't mean that every fag now has a uterus." The Southern drawl in the CO's voice seemed to contaminate the atmosphere with its "good ol' boy" bigotry. "Let's go, Ortega, the goddamn system is setting you free." His final comment was drenched and dripping with despise, as he turned the key to open my cell.

Walking out of that cell for the last time and knowing deep in my heart that I would never return, felt so damn good that I didn't care if that old peckerwood called me a spic. Shit, the way I saw it, I was the one leaving the clink, but that poor old overweight CO would work here until he retired or dropped dead of a heart attack. You see, the dude had no future. His best years were spent harassing prisoners.

Walking out of my cell a free man, I was ecstatic, but the cause of what put me there for twenty-two years still haunted me. It was as if my past was an tormented evil ghost that would rear its grotesque head from the darkest depths of my soul, screaming, "*You will never escape me no matter how hard you try, motherfucker!*" And at that very moment, it had its cold grip around me, bringing with it memories of that fateful day. At that moment, though, I welcomed the bad memory to take over my thoughts right then and there. Shit, at least it helped to drown out the mindless rant of the CO as he escorted me down my final walk down the corridor of Cell Block F.

Making my way down the corridor, I was on autopilot. My body was moving the way any normal healthy body would, but my mind wasn't in the same place as my body. My mind had wandered back to that crisp November night in 1995. I sat in a black Honda Accord waiting for my assignment to arrive, the car's heating system on full blast (I hated the cooler months in Delaware, which made me desire the warmer climate of my beautiful Puerto Rico) as I looked out my car window at the night sky that hung over the streets or Fourth and Lincoln. Héctor Lavoe crooned softly from the car's stereo as I let my mind wander to the objectives of my assignment. I could literally see the bloated face of my boss, Israel Zepeda, as he sat behind his mahogany desk giving me the lowdown on what the assignment was about. "This little shit they call Rico Red is said to be giving intel to the authorities about our family's operation throughout the entire eastern shore of the US, particularly the business we got going down in Miami with the Dominicans and Haitians."

The young boy Rico was supposed to be the representative for the Zepeda family as their distributor of heroin throughout Delaware. In other words, Rico would go down to Miami and pick up an X amount of heroin and bring it up to Delaware via speedboat. It sounds simple enough, right? But no, that stupid little shit put the cops on to the entire operation, so that's where I came in. I was the custodian to clean up their mess. Rico Red had to be dealt with like any other snitch, with a bullet to the head.

The digital clock on my dashboard read 10:45 p.m. when I saw Rico's white Benz park behind my Honda from my rearview mirror, the custom gold Mercedes logo glinting a faint orange glow from the streetlights.

"About fucking time this nigga show up, damn," I said, watching as my target got out of his car. I had to admit, I had no love for Rico and would have gladly done his ass in for free. Shit, the fact that I was getting paid to kill the motherfucker was just a bonus on my view.

I watched him as his red leather-clad body opened the passenger side door to my car and seated himself in the seat. I remember thinking to myself, *Who does this nigga think he is, Eddie Murphy fresh off of his* Delirious *comedy special?*

"What up, man?" said Rico as he gave me dap with a big corny-looking grin plastered on his face.

"Dude, what the fuck is up with that tight-ass red jumpsuit you have on? You look retarded as hell," I scoffed.

"Nigga, why are you hating on me, man? Shit, I gots to look good for the type of money I be pulling in," said Rico in his thick Dominican accent. Truth be told, the dude thought he was hot shit and was very flamboyant when it came to his style. Whether it was the way he dressed or his attitude, dude thought he was big-time, and that was his downfall, so I thought.

"So you're the cat the boss sent to check out the product I picked up from Miami, eh?"

Shocked at the redundant question, I answered, "You see me here driving this car, don't you, dumbass?" As my statement took its full blow on Rico's ego, I looked at him from the corner of my eye. It was then that I became aware of how ridiculous the guy looked.

His hair was fashioned in the style of a pompadour of the early 1960s. His earlobes donned ruby-studded earrings with a pair of ruby-studded sunglasses to match, which glinted each time we passed a streetlamp. "Damn, nigga, who do you think you are? Elton John?" I said this as the bile of disgust began to raise in the back of my throat. That's what I hated most about the young cats coming up in the game when I was in the streets. They would come into a little bit of dough and suddenly they were buying expensive cars, jewelry, and an outlandish wardrobe. Meanwhile, those cats didn't have a pot to piss in because they still lived in their mama's basement, and that was the case with Rico Red.

"Ah, I see how it is, man. You just hating on me 'cause you can't get shit right like me," he said. I could feel Rico's spiteful smile on me as I looked straight ahead as I drove. It was like his cocky smile was digging into me and grating my last nerve.

I am going to enjoy killing this piece of shit, I thought to myself. I drove in silence the entire way to Rico's stash house as he bragged about having two side chicks and a "really good bitch" at home that didn't suspect a thing about his endeavors with the other two woman.

"Yeah, you the man," I said, not really focusing on the garbage he was spewing.

"Dude, turn left right here," said Rico as he pointed toward a self-storage facility off the site of the road.

"Why the fuck do you have the product stashed away in a place like this?" I asked, pulling up to a chain-link security gate that had keypad that stood on a steel pole that was situated right beside it, so when a person drove up, they would be able to punch in their entrance code from the driver's side window. "I'm gonna need your code, man," I said to Rico as I stopped the car in front of the key-pad. "It's one-five-seventy-six," he responded with a huge grin that revealed a set of gold front teeth. "That's my date of birth you just punched in," he said to me with a slight tinge of pride in his voice, as if to convey his cleverness to me.

Jesus, he's just a kid, I thought to myself as I watched the gate slowly open on its pulleys. Oh well, he shouldn't have been playing a grown man's game. He knew what the consequences were if he fucked up. He was just arrogant. These thoughts raced through my mind as my Honda rounded a corner that was filled with what seemed to be small and medium-sized garages stacked side by side like row homes in a ghetto, each with bright orange doors that were complete with padlocks.

"Those three storage containers are where I keep the product," said Rico, pointing out the final three storage sheds to the left of the parking lot. "Just park up to them and then we can get down to business," said Rico.

Was this nigga for real? Was this guy stashing away heroin in a place where there were surveillance cameras? This motherfucker was stupid, no doubt, but I was the one with the dunce cap that night. As it turns out, the kid had on a wire. So when I parked the car and quickly pulled out my gun and shot the bastard through the right temple (at the same time thinking about breaking into the storage facility's main office and stealing the night's surveillance tape), I hear the wailing of police sirens, and suddenly two paddy wagons are blocking my escape, one in the front and in the back. Also, five Delaware State Police cars were blocking the exit to the storage facility. In my moment of desperation, I ran from the car and blacked out.

When I came to, I was in the hospital, hooked up to all kinds of monitors and shit. Apparently, those fucking cops shot me up something serious because I was as in a coma for two and a half months. When I regained my full health back, however, I stood trial and was convicted of murder of the first degree, which my lawyer overturned. It took him twenty-two years, but the man did the damn thing.

"Look alive there, Ortega!" the CO barked, pulling me back to the present.

Shaking the cobwebs from my thoughts, I realized that I was standing in front of a plexiglass window with a slender middle-aged black CO behind it. Boredom seemed to be permanently embedded into his demeanor, his bald head shining from the naked bulb above him. Strangely enough, I could see that the guy's lips were moving, but all I could hear was jumbled mumbling as he handed me the items they had confiscated from me twenty-two years ago.

"Good luck to you, Mr. Ortega," he said, as if he was some ammeter actor who was reading the line from a play in front of handful of people who were attending an acting seminar.

"Thanks, man," I said, my eyes transfixed on the man's shiny head. It was as though he had a halo, and I was drawn to it. I grabbed my bag, watching the man press a button to unlock the exit. Since the exit was on an automatic switch, it slowly flung itself open, releasing what seemed to be compressed air from the electric hinges. Wasting no time, I walked at a brisk pace toward the rectangular ray of sunshine that seemed like a dead body splayed out on the floor. Oddly enough, as I was walking out of that hellhole, I looked behind me and saw my elongated shadow spilled across the floor, swallowing up the sunshine that was once in its place.

CHAPTER TWO

T aking my first steps out of Stone Gate, the first thing that I physically feel is a strong cool wind caressing my face and the backs of my hands, as if it was an old friend welcoming me back home. However, I put all that poetic bullshit out of my mind because the first thing I see when I looked to my left was a 2017 Mercedes SL that had ridiculous-looking chrome-out rims that made me sigh in disgust.

"I swear, cats spend their on the most frivolous things these days," I mumbled under my breath as I moved toward it. The dark green paint job on the car screamed Monday as the morning sunlight bounced off its rims, almost blinding me. The Mercedes logo stood proudly on the car's hood, gleaming in the sun, as if saying, "Yeah, nigga, I got money."

I shook my head at this false symbol of power and wealth. What a false god it was to all of us cats trying to come up in the hood. Shaking my head, I thought, *You know how many dudes I killed inside Benzes like this one right here? Shit, I done lost count of the bodies. The sad thing is, however, the devil ain't gonna let nobody drive a Benz in his hood, you know what I'm saying?*

"What up, Sammy," exclaimed a male voice from the lowered window of the Benz. I walked over to the car and poked my head into the gap that the passenger side window was supposed to occupy. It was then that I realized that my lawyer, Donald Goldman was behind the wheel of that gaudy-looking Benz. Truth be told, I wasn't expecting him to be there, but there he was. Not only was he there, but he was dressed in full street clothes, complete with a black Yankees fitted cap, an oversized white T-shirt, and Timberland boots. From a simple glance, one wouldn't figure the guy driving that Benz to be one of the top criminal lawyers in Delaware, but I guess Goldman was the epitome of the old phrase "Don't judge a book by its cover." Although only thirty years old, Donald Goldman was considered one of the most brilliant lawyers in America, winning the respect of a lot of his colleagues and the hatred of those who opposed him; for those who opposed him knew that he had Mafia and low-level street organizations. Goldman, however, didn't give a fuck what his colleagues thought about him. The way he saw it, they weren't the ones paying his bills and child support.

"What are doing here, man?" I asked, surprised, with a big grin plastered on my face.

"I came to give you a ride in my new joint," he said.

It's funny, but if I closed my eyes at that moment I'd swear I was talking to my homies from around the way. It didn't matter that Donald was a white boy with a Princeton education, he was down as fuck when it came to handling shit. So yeah, dude got his hood pass.

I got in his car, smelling the newness of its cream leather interior as the cool breath of the AC blasted in my face. Shutting the passenger door, I began to notice the heat that started to sting my backside, which forced me to shell out my complaint of Donald's new car. "Damn, nigga, did you really have to get leather seats that are scalding hot in the summer," I whined.

He smiled, pressing Play on the car's CD player. "Quit whining, man, ain't you supposed to be a stone-cold killer?"

I gave him a dirty look as if to say, *"Shut the fuck up, bitch. I will break your face."*

He must have read the look on my face correctly because the smile was instantly gone from his face and replaced with fear. It was then that I got my first taste of twenty-first-century hip-hop music. *"Raindrops drop tops/smoking a splif in a hot box."*

My ears couldn't believe the stupid shit that was coming out of the radio. "Yo, what the fuck is playing on the radio, B?"

Donald looked at me in horror and began to stutter. "Um, it's, ah…Migos."

Ha, I swear, I could literally see the nigga shit his pants. "Dude, is this how all hip-hop music sounds nowadays?" I asked, catching a hint of disparity in my voice and hating it.

"Yup, pretty much, but there are still some truly deep lyricists. For example, you got this cat from Compton who calls himself Kendrick Lamar. There's also another cat that goes by the name of J. Cole, but I forgot what city he reps."

Not caring about much for what he was saying, I asked if he had Nas's *Illmatic*. Without responding to my question, he let out a sigh and said, "Siri, play Nas's *Illmatic*."

At his request, the opening track to *Illmatic* began to play, bouncing off the speakers of the car. "Now that's what the fuck I'm talking about," I exclaimed happily, listening to the track titled "Genesis."

"What's with the shopping bag?" asked Goldman asked, nodding at the Save-A-Lot that rested on the floor of his car.

"Just a little book I wrote," I responded nonchalantly.

"Man, you were steady writing in the clink, huh," said Goldman, with curiosity overtaking him.

There was a moment of silence between us. The only sound in the car was Nas and AZ rapping about how life was a bitch. Clearing his throat nervously, Goldman broke the silence. "You didn't write about your case, did you?" Goldman's voice was filled with apprehension and fear, which caused me to let out a giggle.

"Nah, man, you straight. There ain't nothing about you in my book. That shit just talks about my past in the streets," I said, watching Goldman exhale a sigh of relief. The rest of the ride home was encompassed in a thick silence, which allowed me to go deep into my thoughts

Allowing myself to travel deep into the halls of my psyche, I arrived at a section that housed memories of Sheila Jade, my wife. Just thinking of her mocha-colored skin pressed against mine would drive me to the edge of madness when I was in prison. At night, when sleep failed to sit upon my eyelids, my soul ran wild within the museum of my mind, allowing me to stand in front of portraits of my wife. Yeah, my queen. The one and only woman that could silence the screaming demons that ran wild throughout the valleys of my mind and soul. The woman who noticed that I was human way before I did, or anyone else for that matter. If there's one thing that I thank God for, it's the fact that Sheila is in my life. She has been the closest thing to purity in my life.

"Tell me something, Sammy, how does a stone-cold killer be such a romantic and sensitive poet at the same time?" said Donald, as if reading my mind.

Caught off guard by his comment, I looked at him with an inquisitive glance and said, "What the hell you talking about, bro?"

That's when Goldman's face split into a somewhat grotesque smile and said, "During your last trial, Sheila came to court with composition book full of poems that you had written to her back in the day. My dude, I gotta say, them shits were sappier than a motherfucker. However, I don't blame you. Shit, no offense, but Sheila's sexier than a motherfucker. Man, if my bitch looked like her, I'd be one happy Jewish boy."

Hearing those words come out of his mouth made my blood boil and my fists and jaw clench. I couldn't stand anyone seeing the love of my life as a piece of meat, but I've come to the realization that the reason why some dudes act like that toward women is because they haven't felt the true feelings of being in love, as cliché as that sounds. Yeah, a woman becomes more than a woman when she awakens your heart from a deep dark slumber with her love. Noticing the mixture of anger and disgust on my face, Goldman nervously cleared his throat and quickly changed the subject back to my poetry.

"So how long have been writing?"

By the sound of his voice, I knew that he asked the question out of genuine curiosity and not as a method or tool for clowning me.

"Shit, I've been writing stuff here and there since I was a little runt running crazy in the streets, you know," I said nonchalantly. "Writing down my thoughts and emotions kept me sane. I guess you can say it kept my humanity intact."

Goldman let out a deep sigh and said, "Damn, playa, that's some seriously deep shit, boss."

No more was said between us the rest of the ride home. Nas was the only one talking at the moment, by way of the iPod hooked up to my dude's radio exclaiming that the world was mine.

CHAPTER THREE

As we approached the off ramp of I-95, I could make out the green tiled roof of St. Paul Church, its gray stone facade looking like a castle from the Middle Ages that got sucked into a time portal and dropped smack-dab in the middle of the ghetto. Oddly enough, I always thought of that church as a sign that I was home, a beacon that emphasized the fact that I made it home safely from whatever job or journey I was on.

"Damn, ain't nothing changed about Wilmington the last twenty years, I see!" I exclaimed to no one in particular, eyeing the streets below the interstate where the moving cars and people looked like tiny insects.

"Nah, not much has changed in the city, but they have torn down some old row homes and a few buildings to make room for brand-new town houses. Welcome to the era of gentrification, my friend," Goldman said in a Spanish accent that I found a bit offensive.

"Let me get this straight, the government is tearing down the hood and putting up homes that cost a mint for white people to buy? Ain't that some shit, whites taking back the hood." Shaking my head in disgust, I couldn't help see the irony.

"Come on, man, it's not like the people that lived in those homes weren't paid off by the government," said Goldman defensively.

I couldn't help but shake my head at his response. "No offense, but you are drowning in White Ignorance. Don't you see, even if the government did pay those people off, they still won't give the owner of the house the correct amount the property is worth."

Goldman frowned at this statement and said, "Who died and made you a real estate lawyer?"

I didn't dignify his dumbass question with an answer and just looked out my window, letting my blood simmer down. We were now approaching my block, Fourth and Jackson. The row homes on either side of the block's two sidewalks stood tall, like multiple conjoined twins, giants that were petrified by the passage of time and turned to brick. I could now see the entire left side of St. Paul Church, its stone facade surrounded by a black steel fence that led to an entrance gate to the courtyard.

Damn, that place never changes, I thought. Yup, my ass was definitely home.

"Yo, pull up to the house with the fenced-in front porch," I said to Goldman, pointing out my house. Feeling the excitement surge through my body, I could hardly contain myself, and jumped out the car before it was fully parked.

"Damn, motherfucker, hold your horses," Goldman said between giggles.

Without saying my goodbyes to him, I ran toward the house like a young child coming home on his last day of school. I didn't even make it to the steps when I realized that the front door flew open and Sheila came running down the steps, her silky dark brown hair flowing behind her as she ran toward me. Her torso was hugged tightly by a white tank top, emphasizing her C-cup breasts. I couldn't help but feel my manhood stiffen. She didn't help matters with her tight-ass jeans either. Good God almighty!

Without any formal greeting between us, Sheila ran into my arms, pressing her plump moist lips to mine. I kid you not, we lasted in that particular embrace for at least five minutes. It was as though our bodies and souls hungered for each other. Tears began to stream down our cheeks as we stopped kissing. It was as though our souls were escaping the confines of our bodies to properly greet one another. As if to appease that very desire, I put my tear-streaked face against hers, allowing our fresh tears to mingle, two souls becoming one once again. At that particular moment, the world seemed to fade all around us. It was us, and nothing else in the world mattered. The world could have come crumbling down around us and we would be safe in each other's arms.

"Sammy, don't forget your shit, man!" Goldman yelled from his driver side window, holding out my bag.

As if awaking from a trance, I wiped my eyes and shook the cobwebs from my head, breaking away from Sheila's embrace to run toward Goldman's car. Grabbing the bag from his outstretched hand, I could hear him laughing to himself.

"My dude, you're the softest son of a bitch I know," he said.

"Whatever nigga," I responded, not even giving him a glance as I turned back toward Sheila.

"Have a nice life, Sammy." Goldman's words were barely audible now over the purring of the Benz's engine.

In response to his bland goodbye, I made a peace symbol gesture with my right hand as I walked away.

*****

Entering the house, my sense of smell was overcome with the aroma of Puerto Rican food. My mouth began to water as that smell conjured up images of my favorite food. I knew then that red rice with chickpeas was cooking on the stove, *arroz con gandules* as it is known in Spanish. My stomach began to roar with hunger. It was as though I hadn't eaten in the past twenty-two years. Shit, you gotta understand, I was kept all those years from eating a home-cooked meal. As if in a trance, I let myself be guided by the sweet aroma that was coming from the kitchen. Entering it, I found a short elderly woman in front of the stove, a neat little gray bun sat atop her head. She wore an old yellow flower print dress that seemed to hang loose on her body, as though she had lost a tremendous amount of weight. My heart sank as I suddenly realized who that old woman at the stove was. It was none other than good ole Mami Yadi.

Mami Yadi was the woman who raised Sheila throughout her teenage years, taking her in after the sudden and well-deserved death of Sheila's stepdad. Even though there wasn't any blood relation between the two women, Mami Yadi was the only mother figure the that Sheila ever had in her life. Mami Yadi (Mama Yadi to black kids in the neighborhood) was considered to be the hood's mother, meaning that she fed and even clothed all the kids in the neighborhood. She didn't care if you were black, white, Latin, or a two-headed purple alien from Mars, she showed you all the love in the world. When I was growing up, there was a rumor going around that the reason why Mami Yadi cared for the kids in the neighborhood was because she was barren, which was a shame because she would have been a great mother.

"Mami Yadi, is that you, girl? I said this in a playful tone to generate a reaction from her.

She turned away from the stove with a hand on her hip and gyrating it in a come-hither fashion. "Why, hello there, Sammy, long time no see." She couldn't keep up the joke much longer and stopped her gyration, letting laughter release in the form of a deep hearty bellow. "How are you, *mi amor*?" Mami Yadi asked this as she held out her arms for me to walk into her embrace.

I can't lie, walking into her felt like I was being reunited with my mom after not seeing her for twenty-two years (she visited me once when I was locked up, but I told her not to visit me again because I hated the fact that she had to see me in prison). As a matter of fact, she was the only mother figure I knew growing up. I guess that's what happens when you're found abandoned in a dumpster when you're an infant.

I wasn't adopted by Mami Yadi, though. Instead, I was put in a foster home when I was ten. Don't get it twisted, though; the foster home I grew up in wasn't your average home. It was run by this cat named Carter Johnson. At the time I was there, Carter had at least six kids living in his home, all of whom were males of the black and Latino persuasion. Carter, though, wasn't a fatherly figure. He taught us how to be killers, hustlers, and con artists. He taught me all that there was to be a hit man. Man, Carter would be pissed if he knew how I fucked up Rico Red's murder.

"I see you're still prone to zoning out," Mami Yadi said sarcastically, pulling me away from the memory of Carter.

"What?" I asked a bit disoriented.

"Where's Sheila? I thought I heard her come in the house." I could hear a bit of annoyance start to simmer in her question, which she might have asked numerous times.

"My bad, Mami, I think she's upstairs," I answered her with a smile, hoping that my zoning out didn't piss her off too much.

"*Papito*, do me a favor and tell Sheila that the food's ready," said Mami Yadi as she busied herself at the stove with a frying pan.

Making my way up the second floor, I felt out of place, as if my ass didn't belong there. It was like some surreal feeling within my entire being nagging at me that I didn't belong anywhere., that I should go away and leave Mami Yadi and Sheila alone and not fuck up their lives. As this thought slowly began to fade from my mind, I made my way toward Sheila's bedroom, but I froze in the doorway when I saw her sitting at the foot of the queen-sized bed reading one of my yellow legal pads, with the rest of them beside her. I totally forgot about my book as soon as I entered the house.

"What do you think about it so far?" The sound of my question seemed to shatter the thick silence that encompassed the room.

Without even flinching, baby girl looked at me and said, "Look at you on your Donald Goines shit," she said, getting up from the bed and putting her arms around me.

I let my hands roam around the curves of her body as our tongues danced with one another.

"Let me type that up for you on my laptop, *papi*. I think it has the potential to be a *New York Times* Bestseller," she stated, pumping my ego up.

"You really think so, ma?" I asked, fishing for a response.

"Hell yeah, cats eat that shit up, especially with the title that you gave it."

To be real with you, I thought *Confessions of a Street Soldier* was a wack title for the book, but if Sheila was rocking with it, then it was cool.

CHAPTER FOUR

The smell of sex permeated the walls of the room, drowning out the smell of Mami Yadi's red rice and chickpeas. I lay naked in between the sheets beside Sheila, watching her sleep. Her beautiful face was totally relaxed at the moment, letting me know that she was at peace for now. Although she was thirty-nine years old, ma didn't look a day over twenty-five. Her caramel complexion did not have a single wrinkle. Plus, her body was still on point, rivaling any video vixen out there.

"Puerto Rican don't crack, baby," I whispered to myself, softly giggling. She was my angel, my queen, the whole reason why I still have my humanity.

At that moment, memories of the first time we met began to flood my mind, putting me into the shoes of my thirteen-year-old self on that hot late August at Camby Pool, which was a community pool that kids all over the ghetto frequented every summer until it shut down in the midnineties. That's where me and my nigga Ace would sell weed and make a hell of a profit, too.

"Man, it's hot as hell out here," complained Ace as he took off his plain white T-shirt.

"Shit, you ain't lying, I'm 'bout to jump in that pool my damn self," I replied. I watched as Ace made his way to a row of trees where a bench and a metal trash can were situated under. Hiding what was left of the weed we were selling underneath the trash can, we made our way to the Olympic-sized swimming pool that was teeming with kids.

Noticing that Ace had his shirt draped on one of his shoulders, I decided to bust his balls for a bit. "Dude, ain't you scared of getting sunburned?" I asked.

He responded to me with a snort of laughter. " Nigga, you stupid, don't you know that I have melanin in my skin, which protects me from getting sunburned? That's one of the perks of being dark skinned. Not to mention that dark-skinned niggas been in high demand ever since Wesley Snipes did his thing in *New Jack City.* Shit, bitches can't keep they hands off after they saw that movie. Ha, sometimes I gotta beat the pussy off of me with a stick," bragged Ace, popping an invisible collar from his exposed collarbone.

As if on cue, a chick's voice yelled out, "Ace, don't act like you don't know me, nigga."

Those words froze Ace in his tracks, as if the words were shot from a ray gun that paralyzed every muscle in his body and freezing him in place. Out of nowhere came a beautiful dark-skinned girl and smacked the shit out of Ace, her hand making a grotesque suction sound as it connected with his face.

"Why did you dog me out like that, motherfucker!" the girl cried, her young breasts heaving up and down in anger.

Ace's eyes flooded with anger, but he never advanced toward her. Ace was no saint, by any means, and any other dude would have fucked the chick up really good. Carter, however, taught us well. At that moment, I could literally hear Carter's teaching pass right through his head, as if it were from SoundCloud. "*Despite how much a woman may anger you, never raise a hand to harm her. A man who raises his hand to a woman is nothing but a coward, a bitch-ass nigga. Remember, your hands were made war, but never to bring harm to our queens.*"

"Damn, Chardey, why the fuck you do that for?" cried Ace, his open palms covering his face against Chardey's attacks.

"Nigga, quit acting brand new. You know you fucked up, but what was I expecting from a guy who has a reputation like yours."

As much as I loved Ace, I had to admit that he was somewhat of a dog with the ladies. I had no idea what Ace did to that girl, but more than likely, he got her to fuck him, suck him off, or both. And knowing Ace the way I did, he probably got what he wanted and bounced.

"You ain't nothing but a piece of shit, you inconsiderate bastard!" Chardey yelled at the top of her lungs, almost in a high-pitched squeal. The chick was so angry that her whole body shook uncontrollably, as if she were about to explode. "How could you do that to me, Patrick?"

Ace rolled his eyes, annoyed that Chardey had called him by his real name. "Bitch, why you out here calling me by my government. You should know better than that." Ace said this to her in a tone that sounded like he was an angry father berating his little girl.

Chardey's beautiful facial features were instantly pulled down by the weight of a frown, which strangely seemed to enhance her beauty. I mean, the girl was gorgeous, looking all cute in her two-piece neon red bathing suit.

Truth be told, I wasn't feeling the way Ace was treating Chardey. In my opinion, a chick that beautiful deserved to be treated like a queen, but Ace was the fuck-them-and-leave-them type of dude; that's where him and me differed, but who was I to judge?

"Chardey, what is up with you, girl," said a female's voice as it floated on the wave of an echo in our direction.

I swear, the ears to my soul perked up, causing my heart to awaken from a long slumber. *Where the hell is that beautiful voice coming from*, I thought. My eyes desperately searched the owner of that sweet voice.

"Yo, what is up with you, nigga? You acting all disoriented, like a lost puppy or some shit," exclaimed Ace with a mixture of exasperation and disgust in his voice. Meanwhile, tears were streaming down Chardey's face. "Man, let's fucking bounce," said Ace as we turned our backs on Chardey and started to leave the area.

"Yo, what the fuck y'all do to my girl?"

My heart began to pound in my chest like crazy, as if it was a madman bouncing off the padded walls of his cell. I just had to find out who that beautiful voice belonged to. My heart now controlling the movement of my body, I quickly turned right back around.

Now holding Chardey in a consoling embrace was a mocha-skinned girl in a turquoise one-piece bathing suit. Her hair was long and curly, and when the sun hit it just right, you could see that it was a deep shade of brown. Her eyes were almond shaped, almost catlike, which seemed to bring out the honey brown and a bit of lavender that decorated her irises. Her beautiful pouty lips drove me wild. I had to restrain the urge to kiss them. On the real, I had never in my life seen a girl so beautiful, and I don't care how cliché that shit sounds. Baby girl had a nigga going.

"I asked y'all motherfuckers a question. What did y'all do to my girl?" The question came with more fire and feistiness behind it.

"First off, woman, you need to calm the fuck down," said Ace. His comment seemed to be the lighter fluid that strengthened the flame of her anger. She walked toward him with a sarcastic smile and said between clenched teeth, "I am not your woman!"

Seeing how angry she was, a smile broke the angry scowl that had masked his face. "Chill, ma, you're too pretty to scuffle."

In response to Ace's comment, the girl connected her knee with his groin, causing him to grab himself and howl in pain.

"Let's go. I think we've played enough games with these assholes," said the girl who came to Chardey's rescue, putting her arm around her and walking her away.

"Man, what the fuck you smiling for, nigga," said Ace as he directed his anger at me.

"On the real, my dude, you brought that shit onto yourself," I said in between giggles.

"Yeah, fuck you then, nigga," Ace countered while he retrieved our stash of weed from the metal trash can beside the bench.

"If I didn't know any better, I'd say that your dumbass is in love with that stuck-up little Spanish bitch," he said, giving me the dirtiest look I have ever seen in my life.

"First off, you need to stop playing around with females the way you do. Second, you should know that Spanish broads don't take no shit from nobody."

Ace dismissed what I was saying with a quick "forget you" wave of his hand and laughed. "What you know about that, nigga? You ain't never had no chicks. Come to think of it, I know for a fact that you're still a virgin, nigga," scoffed Ace.

As he made fun of me, I couldn't help wondering what that girl's name was. What was a girl that beautiful doing in a place like Wilmington, Delaware? Don't get a nigga wrong, I'm not saying that my hometown doesn't produce beautiful, but there was something different about this chick that was invading my mind and heart. She was like an exotic creature that was rare to see in this part of the world. For the brief minutes that was our first encounter, my soul was suffering from a divine hunger and thirst so profound, I just had to see her again.

"Yo, dogg, you know that Spanish broad's name?" I asked, interrupting Ace's incessant rambling.

"Ha, I knew it! Bitch got you sprung!"

Hearing him call the girl a bitch infuriated me, causing my teeth to clench and my fists to ball. Word on everything, I was ready to fight that nigga for the first time in our friendship. "Don't call her a bitch, homey," I said, feeling my anger boiling through my veins.

Looking at me from head to toe, Ace scrunched up his face and let out a harsh jeering laugh as he exclaimed, "Nigga, you are so soft that it's ridiculous. Shit, that's not how Carter raised us to be. We're supposed to be street soldiers, men who fight for the betterment of themselves without the binding of any laws whatsoever."

What came to mind at that moment was that Ace had rehearsed that shit he just spewed. It was like he studied Carter's teachings to a tee but didn't put them into practice.

"Ah, but Carter also taught us that we should respect females, for they're our mothers, sisters, and future daughters. Remember, he who doesn't respect females doesn't respect life itself because females are the portals of all human life. In other words, without women, we wouldn't exist. Therefore, we owe them the ultimate respect." I wasn't just saying that. I spoke from the heart, and Ace knew that.

"Whatever, nigga, you're just saying that because that Spanish chick got your dick all hard and shit." Ace said this as he opened the front door to our house where we lived with Carter, our foster father, on the eleven hundred block of Lancaster Avenue.

Ace carried on with his jeering until we came in the front door and saw Carter sitting across the living room on the old rose-print sofa, the kind that is usually associated with an old lady's home. He sat in the middle with his legs open, sporting black basketball shorts with a white tank top embossed with a neon red Nike logo. His hairless dark brown scalp shone brilliantly against the light fixture above his head, making him look like some of hood saint.

"What are you little niggas babbling about?" Carter asked, taking his attention away from the book he was reading and focusing it on us.

"Sammy's in love," said Ace in a high-pitched girly voice, batting his eyes.

I could feel my face begin to redden, thinking that Carter would view me as weak for expressing emotions. Instead, to my surprise, Carter's face split into a grin, one that seemed to mimic the smile of that creepy feline from *Alice in Wonderland*. His eyes shone with glee, as if he had spent years yearning to witness one of his foster children to fall in love. However, his smile faded as quickly as it spread on his face.

"Y'all little niggas got my money?" Carter asked this question with the seriousness of a doctor that was telling his patient that they had cancer.

"Yeah, man, we got your dough," said Ace, his voice sounding with a deep timber of confidence while digging in his jeans pockets and handing Carter a wad of money.

As the money was being placed in the palm of his hand, I could see Carter's eyes scrutinizing the size of the money stack. "Y'all niggas came up a bit short today, huh?" Despite his slight disappointment, however, he pocketed the money and released a sigh of disgust.

Seeing this, Ace began to transform into defensive mode, explaining why the wad of cash was so low. "Man, you know them little shits at Camby Pool ain't got nothing but fucking milk money. Shit, we're lucky if we get a customer that spends twenty dollars on this shit!" Ace yelled with the full force of anger that he seemed to hold back during his argument with Chardey and the Spanish chick.

The dark cloud of a scowl took over Carter's face, as if he was a sniper positioning the little red dot of his rifle on his target.

Without a single word, Carter jumped from the sofa and punched Ace square in the jaw, causing the boy to reel back and fall to the floor, holding his jaw.

"You better come correct when you step to me with all that crazy back talk, boy!"

Wide eyed with fear and shock, Ace got on his feet and walked up to Carter with his head down, mumbling that he was sorry. Carter nodded his head in response to Ace's apology, as if to say that he was forgiven for his rudeness. Still holding the left side of his jaw, Ace walked upstairs to the room we both shared.

"Sammy, go upstairs and try to talk some sense into Ace. That little nigga has lost his goddamn mind. Little shit is feeling himself, huh?"

Without saying a word, I headed upstairs and directly to my room. As soon as I entered, I was greeted by the sound of a punching bag being hit repeatedly by what sounded like rapid punches. On the real, though, I could have cared less about Ace's current issue with Carter. Ace was always getting himself into shit. Man, most of the time he got what he deserved.

"Carter be on some bullshit!" Ace whined as he pounded heavily on the punching bag. "Nigga better slow his roll, you know what I'm saying?"

On the real, though, my ass didn't care what he was saying. I was too preoccupied with thoughts of Chardey's homegirl. My mind kept going back to her feisty attitude and the way she defended Chardey against Ace's rudeness. Hell, I loved witnessing that, a strong-minded Spanish broad. Shit, at the time, the Spanish broads that I encountered were usually overly submissive with men, obeying the will of just about every man that they came across. That wasn't the case with this chick, however. Nah, this one wasn't going to lie down and let dudes trample all over her. She was going to let herself be heard, felt, and feared. Goddamn, that is some kind of broad. Shit, I just knew right then and there that I needed to be with her, surrounding myself with the beauty that was her. On the real, I thought love was some fairy-tale shit that you see in a fucking Disney flick, but that hot August day in 1990 gave me a whole new perspective on what love and the courage of a strong-minded female really were. As cliché as that might sound, that was my introduction to love, making a human being.

As the summer drew on, I had no contact whatsoever with the Spanish beauty that was now the queen of my heart. Every day I would go to Camby Pool, making my rounds, selling weed and checking for my queen, but she was nowhere to be found, which would send my mind into full on poet mode.

"Nigga, you need to erase that bitch from your mind. Otherwise, you're going to make yourself sick in the head." Ace would say this whenever he would see me writing a poem at my desk.

Of course, I would shake off his comments because I knew that he didn't know what it felt like to be in love.

"Nigga, that ain't love, that is called obsession."

I shook my head defiantly without turning away from what I was writing and said, "If you only open the doors to your heart, you would know exactly how I feel."

Sucking his teeth, Ace responded, "Man, fuck all that faggot bullshit you be on," he said, storming out the room.

One night, as I was finishing up my umpteenth love poem of the summer, Carter walked in and pulled up a chair beside me. He wore a white wifebeater with a pair of baggy jeans and Timberland boots. His forearms bulged, showing the signs of a dude who lifted a large number of weights on a daily basis. "Little nigga, what's this I hear about you tripping over some chick you met at Camby's?"

Carter's question caught me a bit off guard, which must have showed on my face because he had a grin on his face that reminded me of Ace when he knew a big secret and wasn't telling me.

"I don't know what you're talking about, man," I said, thinking I could get one past Carter. That's when his right fist came out of nowhere and connected with my jaw, knocking me to the floor.

"Why you gotta lie to me, nigga!" He seemed to form a sonic blast as he stood over me. Trying to stop my head from spinning, I managed to pick myself up off the floor and stand before him with the burning coals of anger shining brightly in my eyes. "Oh, so you pissed now, huh," Carter mocked as he got into a fighting stance. "Come at me then, nigga," he said, fanning the flames of my anger. Shit, I knew what time it was.

Suddenly, Carter came at me with the fury of a hurricane, forcing me to duck to prevent from getting a swift kick to the head. He then proceeded to attack with a succession of rapid punches to my body and face, which I expertly blocked. Noting that there was an opening to attack his midsection, I let of a succession of punches, knocking the wind out of Carter. Noticing that he was in a daze, I quickly jumped up and connected to swift roundhouse kick to Carter's face, causing him to land hard on my desk, which caved in on its four legs. Watching my desk collapse under Carter was the shit to me. It meant that from that moment on, I was to be respected by him, and it also meant I was officially a man that could hold my own in this cold cruel world.

Walking toward his laid-out body, I braced myself for anything, keeping my guard up. Knowing that motherfucker like I did, I was prepared for any unexpected attack that he would most likely throw at me.

"Rule number one," Carter would often say during our training, "don't underestimate your opponent when he's down. Remember, your opponent will use the fact that he is down to lure you in for a sneak attack, killing you in the process. Always keep your guard up no matter what."

Shit, and best believe that my ass took that to heart at that moment I was walking up to his sprawled body on that broken desk. To my surprise, though, he didn't sneak attack me. Instead, he smiled at me, looking like some hungover vampire with extremely bloody fangs.

"Damn, little nigga, I taught you well," said Carter, his hand on his lower back, trying miserably to relieve the pain. "Let me get cleaned up and we'll talk about this chick that got you going all crazy," he said while rubbing his lower back, slowly walking out of my room, as if he was a decrepit old man that was hunched over.

After getting cleaned up and in his blue terry cloth robe, Carter met with me at the dining room table, a small wooden round thing that seemed to symbolize the poverty that we were living in, with scuff marks on that seemed to suggest that it had seen better days. We didn't care, though. Shit, that was the table that we told our secrets at. Many a person's fate was decided at that table. Hell, even blood and pieces of brains were splattered on its surface every once in a while, but at that particular moment, that table was holding count of matters of the heart.

Carter sat down in one of the rickety old wooden chairs that served as a seat for the dining room table. It creaked under his weight. "What's this I hear about you falling head over heels over some little broad you met at Camby's?" Carter asked, stone-faced, making me scared to answer. "Look, don't get me wrong, it's cool to fall in love, but you can't let it blind you to the point of obsession. Once you do that, you will become weak in all aspects of your person, meaning that if you obsess over love, your mind, body, and spirit will become distorted, allowing your enemies to overrun you and take what is yours. Remember that I raised you to be a soldier because we are in battle with this white man's world, so I raised you to get by in it by any means necessary. Shit, even if it means that you gotta catch a body. Don't let that little chick be your downfall. Don't let her be the Eve to your Adam. You understand what I'm saying to you, nigga?"

"I get what you're saying, but I never thought that that any human emotion like this ever existed," I said, causing Carter to give me a strange look. Taking notice of this, I continued to expand my point. "I know this shit that I am telling you might sound cliché, but just the sound of that girl's voice seemed to cleanse my soul. It was as if at that moment when her voice struck my eardrums, my heart was awakened from a deep slumber and showed me that there was a part of me that was missing. Do you know what I mean, man?"

Carter nodded his head solemnly, letting each word I said sink in. That was when I noticed a single tear drop sliding down his left cheek, shocking the fuck out of me. Seeing him cry for the first time was like watching a god break down at my feet. Shit like that never happened. Carter was a cold-blooded killer who dedicated his life to molding future killers. He wasn't the type of nigga that showed his emotions. He was the type of cat to use his emotions as fuel to enhance physical training to become a better killer.

"You see this damn tear coming down my cheek?" Carter asked, keeping his voice steady. Still in shock, I didn't know how to answer him. "This tear coming down my cheek is my soul trying to escape this wretched body of mine to steal the love that you have discovered." After saying this, he got up from his chair and went upstairs, leaving me in shock at the dining room table. Now, although what Carter said to me was a bit dramatic, know that the dude was a self-educated man that read mostly Shakespeare plays and thick English novels from the eighteenth and nineteenth centuries. That's why the dude would express himself so deeply. I'm talking about a guy who would read us Sun Tzu's *The Art of War* as part of our daily kung fu lessons. Shit, you couldn't catch him anywhere without a book in his hands.

As I left the dining room and made my way upstairs, I could hear the soulful sound of the Isley Brothers' song "Drifting on a Memory," which came from Carter's room. Making my way down the narrow hallway, I noticed that the door to his room was slightly ajar and the light was on. With curiosity pushing me forward, I stood outside the door with one eye looking into the thin opening. That was when I saw Carter wrapping a blanket above his forearm tightly, causing a vein to bulge out and injecting it with heroin. His tears were now sliding down his cheek in thick streams, reminding me of a burst dam. It was at that moment that I saw a god crumble and destroy himself before my eyes.

With school starting up the following week and no sign of the girl from Camby Pool, I had decided to strictly focus on my training. Plus, I found that in some fucked-up way, my kung fu training with Carter helped to block out the image of him injecting heroin into himself. There wasn't a moment during our training that he looked like he was strung out. Shit, the dude was flawless during training, which made it easier for me to forget that he was using heroin. I never told anyone about Carter's addiction, not even Ace.

On the first day of school, me and Ace were standing outside the front doors to Alexis I. DuPont High School. Bored out of our minds waiting for the doors to be unlocked, we started to talk shit about how the school year was going to turn out for us. "Man, watch me holla at the flyest bitch in here," said Ace, seeming to transform that statement into a high school boy's cliché.

I smiled, trying to show interest in what Ace was saying, but I wasn't feeling it.

"Yo, what's your problem, nigga? You high or some shit?" Ace said, noticing that I was only half listening to what he was saying.

"Nah, man, just thinking about school, is all."

Ace scrunched up his face, which let me know that he didn't believe a word I was saying. On the real, I was getting tired of Ace's immature ways and how he treated women. I know we were young back then, but that wasn't an excuse to go breaking hearts. Plus, I partly blamed him for possibly screwing up my chances with Chardey's homegirl. "Man, I'm good, just thinking is all." I said this in the hopes that Ace would get off my back.

"Shit," Ace said with a hint of despair in his voice.

I turned my head toward the direction he was looking at and saw Chardey talking with the Spanish chick that stole my heart at Camby Pool a few weeks earlier. She was rocking a jet-black spandex suit with a royal blue zigzag line that ran down her right thigh. She also wore washed-out jeans with a sown-on Puerto Rico flag on one of the breast pockets. Letting my eyes roam the length of her body, I noticed that she had on a pair of black Reebok Classics to complete her look. Her ears glistened in the early morning sunlight, as her large gold hoop earrings caught the light. Man, but what caught my attention the most was her beautiful long brown hair cascading down her back. Such beauty was like a magnet, and I was drawn by it. At that particular moment, I can't remember what Ace and me were talking about because I just left him talking by himself and made my way toward Chardey and her homegirl. Feeling the butterflies fluttering in my stomach, my throat began to tighten. I feared that I wouldn't be able to talk, but to my surprise, I was able to say a soft hello before my nerves took over.

Hearing my voice, both girls turned to face me. As soon as they saw me, though, their faces scrunched up into disgust, as if I was a piece of dog shit they had stumbled upon unexpectedly.

"Who the fuck said you could come over here?" asked Chardey's homegirl, seeming to remember the I was the homey of the dude that broke Chardey's heart.

"Chill, ma, I just wanted to say, 'What's up.'"

Both girls rolled their eyes in unison and walked away. Chardey then giggled as she walked away with her friend. "Damn, Sheila, that was harsh," said Chardey as both girls turned their backs on me, heading for the main entrance of the school.

On some real shit, though, I didn't feel disrespected. Nah, quite I felt quite the opposite. I felt happier than a motherfucker cause I finally knew the Spanish broad's name. That entire day, the sound of her name rang throughout my head like a damn ear worm. My heart would beat wildly against my chest every time I would whisper her name. *Ah, Sheila.* The very thought of her made my knees weak.

Now, I know niggas will be like, "Man, that motherfucker Sammy is soft as shit. That pussy-ass bitch ain't no gangster!" But to those that think that way, fuck'um. On some real shit, we are all human and need love to sustain us. Unfortunately, though, shorty wasn't feeling the same way at the time. Although Sheila and me had most of our classes together, we didn't speak to one another because she would avoid me at all costs, all thanks to Ace's dumb ass. I knew I had to show her that I wasn't like Ace at all. I had to show her that I knew how to treat a lady, but how? At times, I would literally find myself talking to God, asking Him to please help me find a way that I could steal Sheila's heart. On the real, I would find myself crying my eyes out, asking God to help me find a way. As crazy as this might sound to nonbelievers, God did help me find a way to win Sheila's heart in the form of poetry.

In mid-November of that year, the English department of our school was hosting a poetry slam. For those that wanted to sign up, they were directed to a sign-up sheet that was posted outside the cafeteria. One day, just out of curiosity, I started to look over the names on the list, and lo and behold, I found Sheila's name. Taking out my pen from my back pocket, I quickly scribbled my name under hers and walked away.

Coming home from school that afternoon, I ran up to my room and quickly began to write a poem that went a little something like this:

Her beautiful ancestry flows upon her flesh
Like a majestic river, giving life to Taino Indian queen
That bathes in the pools of her eyes, cleansing her
soul.
If I look close I am able to appreciate the fine
Architecture of the edifice that houses her soul;
One that was fashioned by her great African
Ancestry, sculpting her hip and thighs
Just right.
Meanwhile, she stands with the elegant grace of the
queen of Spain.
Oh, how I hunger to touch my lips to hers, making
them pilgrims to
A new land; a land so foreign to me, that touching
it would result in my being destroyed, only to be
renewed in the essence of love.

The next day after school, my ass sat in a sweltering auditorium listening to five or six suicide poems that all seemed to sound the same. On the real, I was bored out of my fucking mind, Shit, I was about ready to bounce without reading my poem—until Sheila's name was called.

Man, she looked so sexy walking to the stage in her tight jeans, Timberlands, and a tight fitted short-sleeved T-shirt that didn't leave any room to the imagination. I can't say that I was all ears when she was reading her poem, but she definitely had my attention. Like I said before, her beauty was mesmerizing, and I was in a whole other world whenever she was around me.

After a few minutes of being in my little trance, the sound of my name being called seemed to shatter that trance and bring me back to reality. I got up from my seat with my back stiff and my poem in hand. Making my way up the stage, I can honestly say that I didn't feel an ounce of nervousness. I look at that moment like it was one of those times where I had to prove myself during training with Carter. There was no room for chickening out.

I made my way up to the mic and said, "This poem is dedicated to Sheila Jade," and just did the damn thing. I was in the zone at that moment, and when I was done reciting my poem, I walked off the stage, pulling the hood from my sweatshirt on my head, exiting the auditorium.

In the hallway, making my way toward the exit of the back lobby, I was halted in my tracks by a girl calling my name. Turning around, I came face-to-face with Sheila. "Did you really mean what you said in your poem?" she asked, as hope shimmered in her eyes.

My heart was beating a mile a minute. It took a second for me to respond. "Yeah, everything I said in that poem is what's in my heart," trying to sound nonchalant about the matter. "I've been feeling you ever since that day I first saw you at Camby's."

Her expression seemed to soften at my confession, as if I had penetrated an invisible shield that guarded her emotions. "Well, I'm sorry I dogged you out, but I had to defend my girl. Ace was an asshole to her."

On the real, I didn't give a fuck what she thought about Ace, at least she was talking to me at the moment. "Man, I feel you. Don't even worry about it. I know how Ace can be sometimes," I said, shaking my head, hoping that I didn't sound like one of those dudes that would say anything to get in a girl's pants, even if it meant throwing their best friend under the bus.

After what seemed like an awkward pause, Sheila cleared her throat and said, "I wouldn't mind hanging out sometime." She said this as she looked bashfully down at her feet, her cheeks reddening a bit.

"Yeah, I'm down for whatever," I responded, a bit too overzealous.

Reaching into her into her back pocket, she produced the paper she had written her poem on and a pencil, scribbling on it very rapidly. "Here's my number," she said, handing me the piece of paper. Sheila's phone number was written neatly with smiley faces and hearts circling it. "Call me, okay. Maybe we can chill on Saturday," said Sheila, walking back toward the auditorium.

"I'll see you around," I said, watching her hips sway back and forth as she entered the auditorium.

In the weeks that followed, Sheila and me were inseparable. Of course, I soon discovered that Sheila wasn't stuck up like Ace thought. As a matter of fact, she was exactly the opposite. This might have been because I was biased at the time, but Sheila was the most down-to-earth broad I have ever seen in my life. I never heard her bad-mouthing or beefing with other chicks, and I never saw her fronting whenever we were together and there were cats from school around. She was always herself, a genuine heart. I also found out that she was a huge anime nut. I could sit and watch her draw *Sailor Moon*, *Golgo 13*, and *Speed Racer* for hours. We also would spend our time together walking around the whole Hilltop section of Wilmington, talking about our favorite poets our favorite genre of music. I could tell from the amount of time that we were spending together that she was feeling me as much as I was feeling her, so I kissed her smack-dab on the lips, letting mine linger on hers for what seemed like eternity. When she didn't pull from me in disgust, I knew that she liked it. Releasing from our kiss, she put her head on my shoulder and whispered, "I love you, Sammy." As Sheila's words sank into my heart, I could feel the cipher of my humanity completing itself.

Stepping out of that memory of Sheila and me and placing it back on the gallery of my mind, my thoughts returned to the present, where I was lying next to Sheila as she slept. Kissing her forehead, I said a little prayer, thanking God for letting me be reunited with my queen. It was at that moment that I realized that was the first time I had spoken to God in twenty-seven years. Ironically the two conversations I had with God came full circle, both having to do with Sheila.

"I will burn in hell before I let anything happen to you," I vowed in a low whisper that was barely audible as I kissed her forehead once again.

CHAPTER FIVE

In the weeks following my release, I tried to keep my nose clean, but for motherfuckers like me, it is virtually impossible to stay out of trouble. Lord knows that I tried going the straight and narrow path, but once a nigga gets a taste of the streets, it's very hard to let that shit go. Don't get me wrong, the first week I was out of prison, I got a regular nine-to-five job. Mami Yadi was nice enough to get me hooked up with a job a Dominican bodega on Fourth Street, across from the old Latin American Community Center, but I just wasn't feeling it. Man, what I look like working as a damn stock boy at some bodega? Shit, I was a millionaire when I was working with the Zepeda crew. Now look at me, with a Kelly green apron on and stocking fucking mangoes.

Sheila would notice my disappointment when I would come home from work and say, "Cheer up, *papi*. Book is gonna sell and then you don't have to work at that bodega anymore."

The funny thing was that I would completely forget that she was done typing my book and had sent it off to a bunch of publishers who had swiftly rejected it. "Ma, ain't nobody gonna publish my shit. It's too hood," I said, raising my voice in frustration.

"Oh, I know you ain't talking to me like that, nigga," she said, turning from her position at the kitchen sink and getting up in my face. "Your ass ain't the only one adjusting to this new change. You gotta realize that even though my love for you never wavered in the past twenty years, I have to get use to the fact of physically having you here with me. Hell, there are times that I wake up at and the shit is scared out of me because I am not used to having you by my side late at night. Or the times when you come home from work early and you come up from behind me on your tippy toes and kiss me on the neck. That frightens me to death because I am not expecting you. But you don't see me getting rowdy with you. That's just something I have to work through, so please don't make this transition hard on me."

I stood in the middle of the kitchen for a couple seconds, letting her words sink in. I ain't gonna lie, Sheila's words were like daggers to my heart, but she was being real with me. I had to respect that. I was at a loss for words at the moment, so I went to the front porch to sit on a rickety old lawn chair to smoke a blunt. If there was one thing that I hated the most about the ghetto, it's the fact that you can't see the stars at night because of the damn streetlights. So I sat back with my blunt hand envisioning the stars, which may see us humans as imperfect gods crumbling in the wind.

As these thoughts flowed through my mind, I failed to noticed the presence of Ace walking up to my porch. I only became aware when I realized that a shadow was looming over me, blocking the faded orange glow from the streetlight that stood in my direction.

"What up, nigga? Long time no fucking see," Ace said, but for some reason, my brain couldn't register that it was his voice. Shit, that must have been some good-ass weed for that to happen. "Yo, wake up, nigga!"

Getting annoyed with the damn shadow barking orders at me, I looked up at its face and realized that it was Ace. "Oh shit, my dude, what's happening," I yelled excitedly, getting up from my chair to embrace my brother.

I hadn't seen Ace in a minute. Last time I saw him was at Carter's funeral in 1994. After Carter's death, Ace and me went our separate ways. I stayed with the Zepeda crew while Ace did his shit with the drug game down in Miami, which I heard made him rich beyond his wildest dreams. So what was he doing back here in Delaware, I wondered.

We broke from our brotherly embrace and sat down, Ace taking the lawn chair beside me all cool and nonchalant in his white

Sixers jersey with the fitted cap to match. "I heard you was doing life, nigga," said Ace, sparking up a conversation.

"Yeah, that's true, man, but I beat the case off of some crazy-ass loophole in the legal system that my lawyer found," I said, taking a puff from my blunt.

"Shit, that must have been a hell of a lawyer to have found that loophole 'cause your ass was buried. I mean, it seemed that the only way you were getting out of prison was via body bag," Ace said as he reached for my blunt. "Aye, man, don't be stingy. Pass the duchy on the left hand side," said Ace, mocking a Jamaican accent.

I smiled, passing him the blunt and continuing my explanation about how I got out of prison. "Shit, for a while there, I thought that I was going to die in that hellhole, but Sheila fired my old lawyer and got me this young cat by the name of Donald Goldman. I swear, nigga is a fucking genius," I said, with conviction ringing in my voice.

Releasing a thick clouds of marijuana smoke both from his mouth and nostrils, Ace looked like a humanoid dragon getting ready to breathe fire on an unsuspecting village, which brought a smirk to my face.

"Nigga, what are you smiling for?" asked Ace suspiciously as he looked at me.

"Did you know your ass always looks like some kind of weird dragon whenever you smoke?"

Hearing this statement, Ace gave me the side eye and said, "Nigga, I think you smoking something else besides the weed in this blunt. Anyway, nigga, I ain't come here to chitchat like two old ladies." Ace took another puff from the blunt then continued. "I came out here to ask you a favor," he said, looking me dead in the eye.

It was then that I felt the darkness awaken within me, shaking itself off from a deep twenty-two-year slumber. I could feel it sitting up and licking its chops, waiting for its time to feed. Mind you, I would only feel this darkness awakening in me when it was time for me to kill. It was like a strange craving I couldn't control. I had to satisfy it immediately or go insane. Oddly enough, however, Ace asking me for a favor was the thing my darkness needed to awakened, and it was damned happy to be awake. You see, when Ace gets right down to the point in a conversation, that usually meant that heads were going to roll and blood was going to flood the motherfucking streets. Don't get it twisted, when I got out of prison, I vowed to walk a straight and narrow path, but when shit pops off and my brother Ace needs me, I am down for whatever the cause. Family over everything, that's what Carter taught us.

The front porch grew thick with silence, as if it was a heavy Afghan quilt that was suddenly draped over us. It wasn't hard to tell that Ace was choosing his words carefully before he spoke. I could literally see when his mind chose what he was going to say. On the real, dude's face indicated that what he was going to tell pained him to a certain extent.

Ace cleared his throat before he spoke. "We gotta take Zepeda out, nigga." Ace blurted that shit out so quickly that I hardly understood what he had said. He must have seen the confused look on my face because he repeated what he said more clearly. "This ain't no joke, man. That fucking fat bastard is trying to muscle in on my coke and heroin business down in Florida, and a nigga ain't having that, you feel me?"

I sat there listening, trying to piece it all together. "Wait, I always thought that Zepeda had Miami on lock," I stated, confused as shit.

"Damn, nigga, I didn't know you was that far out the game!" Ace said angrily, as if I should have known better. Releasing a sigh of disappointment, Ace began to speak. "Back in the early 2000s, me and that fat fuck Zepeda had an agreement. We had both agreed that anything south of Miami was my turf and anything north of Miami was his, including the whole East Coast of the United States. Nah, but nigga had to be greedy. He sent his niggas up to my most lucrative trap houses, killed a ton of my soldiers, and made off with at least a hundred thousand dollars. That motherfucker gotta get dealt with," Ace said, anger flaming every word he was saying.

I couldn't believe what I was hearing. Shit, back in the day, Zepeda was nothing but good to us. That dude made us both millionaires, so you can imagine why I had to give my man the side eye. "Dude, are you sure about this?" I said, still trying to grasp what Ace was saying.

"Nigga, what I look like coming at you with a lie like that for? It's even an insult that you would ask me some stupid shit like that. As a matter of fact, peep this out, nigga," he continued, adding renewed vigor to what he was saying. "Zepeda is the reason you was locked up all them years. The cops was putting pressure on about the drugs he was selling because they want some more of his hush money. So when the fat bastard said no, that's when the cops threatened to raid all of his stash houses, which included putting word to the FBI about his dealings in other states. So what did the nigga do? He had your ass set up by Rico Red, except that Rico dying wasn't part of the plan."

I was taken aback by this revelation, I couldn't believe what I just heard. I didn't want to believe it, as matter of fact. "Yo, who gave you information?" I said angrily.

Now it was Ace's turn to be shocked. "Nigga, what are you talking about? Everybody knows about that shit. Fuck, I'm surprised that you didn't find that out in the clink."

As Ace was telling me all this, my mind started to crank out memories of my time in prison that I kept buried deep down the dark recesses of my subconscious, bringing about the haggard features of a man that had been severely scarred on his face. The scary thing was that the scars on this dude were done in weird shapes, as if a small child had done them. One of the scars on the man's face resembled a smiley face that was on his left cheek in the form of a crude, jagged circle with a pair of eyes and a mouth that resembled a half moon. The dude even had stick figures on his face that seemed to dance every time he would say to me, "Zepeda set you up, man!"

I ain't pay him no mind, though, because I thought that the guy was a nut, with his neo-Nazi tattoo on his forehead and his shaved head gleaming in the prison lights. The guy would constantly approach me every chance he got and repeat his claim about Zepeda. He would do this every day until he was found dead in an unused stairwell with a shiv sticking out of the left side of his neck.

Looking back at it now, in connection to what Ace had revealed to me, it seemed that someone wanted to silence the dude before he said too much.

With this thought eating away at me like strong acid eating through metal, I was now fully convinced that Zepeda and his crew needed to be taken out. Fuck living a normal life this was personal. That fat fuck kept me away from Sheila for twenty-two years, keeping me from my whole life. It is because of him that I never had the chance to start a family with Sheila in our younger years. To top the shit off, she was pregnant when I was arrested. The stress of my situation caused her to have a miscarriage. Yo, word on everything, that piece of shit was going down.

"I'm in, dog," I said without giving it any more thought.

Hearing my response seemed to activate a noticeable sense of confidence in Ace. It was as though a thousand pounds were lifted from his shoulders, causing him to relax. "I knew I could count on you, man," he said, giving me dap. "Meet me at Silverbrook Cemetery tomorrow at eight in the morning by Carter's gravesite," he said, getting up from his chair and heading down the porch steps. "It was nice seeing you," he called out without looking back at me and heading toward the direction of St. Paul School.

As he walked under a street light, I noticed that it flickered a faint orange glow and abruptly went out, leaving Ace to look like a dark featureless silhouette roaming the night.

CHAPTER SIX

S itting there on the porch, my mind was at war with itself. Every fiber of my being wanted me to go after Zepeda in full force, but I also had to think about the consequences going after an individual like Zepeda would entail. Attacking his entire organization meant that his associates would come after us guns blazing, which meant cutting a deal with them ahead of time, letting them know what was going to happen to Zepeda's organization and then trying to get those associates on our side. That was going the hardest shit we had to do. That was my biggest concern about the situation. Shit, Zepeda had connections with all types of Mafia fighters all over the country, including both Jewish and Yakuza connections.

"What the fuck did I get myself into," I asked aloud to the cool autumn night that was encompassing me.

Getting up from the lounge chair and making my way inside the house, a dark force seemed to grab hold on my mind. It was as if my past as a hit man wanted to remind me of something, its cold fingers wrapping itself around my mind and pulling me toward a memory that I had thought lay buried in my unconscious.

The memory was of Sheila crying alone with her back against her locker, which was our usual meeting spot when we skipped study hall. As I made my way toward her, she kept turning her head in the opposite direction, as if trying to avoid looking at me.

"What's up with you, ma?" I asked, taken completely off guard by the way she was acting toward me. It was as though she was a puppy that didn't want to be touched by anyone. I placed my hand on he to turn her toward me, causing her to jolt in fright, as if my very touch had stung her severely. I could feel the sky falling on me at that point. Sheila never was afraid of me, I had never given her reason to be. I gently moved her head toward me so I could look directly into her eyes. That was when I noticed that she had a black eye, along with what seemed like a sea of blood in the white of her right eye, which meant that one of her blood vessels in her eye had burst.

"What the hell happened to your eye, ma?" I asked while rage was coursing through my veins.

With fear in her eyes, she told me everything. It was like witnessing a dam bursting open. "I got into a fight with my dad," she said in between sobs. "He told me to stop seeing you, and when I refused, he beat me." As the last of her words left her mouth and sank into my heart, I punched the locker beside her, leaving a huge dent on its door that caused a loud clang, which echoed throughout the halls like a metallic groan of pain. It wasn't news to me that Sheila's pops didn't want me to see her. The motherfucker hated my guts. You would think that her pops was just being your run-of-the-mill overprotective father, but there was something much sinister about their relationship. It was by those lockers that she confessed to me that her pops was raping her on a nightly basis. The rage that was coursing through my veins had reached its boiling point to the point I had decided to take matters into my own hands.

"Sheila, everything is going to be all right, I promise," I said to her in a soft voice, trying to get my rage under control. I knew what to do then. It was time to get vengeance for Sheila, and I would call upon Ace for his assistance in the matter. "Everything's going to be okay, baby," I repeated before walking toward the exit.

A few hours later, I caught up with Ace and told him all that went down with Sheila and her pops.

"Oh yeah, I know that, nigga. He chills at the whorehouse down on route thirteen. Nigga be frontin' like a motherfucker, too. He's always telling the girls that he got mad stack when everybody knows that he's fucking broke, but the bitches like to humor him," said Ace, letting out a little chuckle as he puffed on a blunt.

The reason why he knew that information about Pops was because he was working for Zepeda as security at the whorehouse, which by all intents and purposes should have been illegal as fuck (Ace was fourteen at that time, but physically he resembled a twenty-four-year body builder), but he had the law in his pocket and could do whatever he pleased.

"Dude, that is perfect. I could wet him up right there on the spot. You think Zepeda will get salty if we use his spot to body that piece of shit?" I said, frustration oozing out of every fiber of my being.

Ace snorted in amusement at my question and said, "Fuck no, that fat bastard would be happy as hell if you got rid of Sheila's pops. That nigga owes him like a million dollars that we all know he ain't gonna pay back. Shit, you'll be doing the boss a favor. Matter of fact, I'll take you to go see Zepeda at one of his joints so that you can tell him about your situation."

So it was settled. Ace set up a time and place where I was to meet Zepeda the next day.

Skipping school the next day, Ace and I set out to meet with Zepeda at one of his businesses, which was a run-down laundromat on Maryland Avenue that sat in the middle of a shopping area that seemed to be forgotten by time. Most of its stores had gone out of business since the late 1970s, and what remained were little mom-and-pop shops that were barely staying afloat.

Entering the laundromat, the smell of Clorox and other liquid detergents assaulted my nose, causing me to hold my breath. On the real, if I hadn't done that, I would have thrown up all over my damn self.

"Just act cool, nigga. Stop acting like you scared or some shit. Wipe that worried look off your face too. The dude can smell fear, and believe me, if he does, your ass will be invisible to him. It will be like you never even existed, so man the fuck up, nigga!" Ace said this as we took a seat on a couple of metal folding chairs that were situated in front of a picture window that looked out onto the parking lot of the shopping center.

We sat in silence for what seemed like an eternity, watching the diverse clientele of the laundromat go through the motions of the mundane task of washing clothes. It was as though every individual in that place was a part of a fine-tuned machine that kept the laundromat alive. Every once in a while, the occasional crackhead would come up to where we were sitting and ask we had any spare change, but Ace would quickly shoo them away as if he were a dog owner who was fed up with his pet's shenanigans.

We had been waiting so long there that I began to observe a woman that seemed to have been battered and beaten by time itself. Her face was so sallow and wizened that it seemed to resemble dried-up riverbeds. Her body was paper thin without a single curve in sight, making her white tube top and baby blue short shorts cling to her body, which made her look like a human scarecrow. On the real, the bitch was fucking freaky looking, especially her eyes, which seemed sunken deep into her skull. Shit, it was no wonder that when she spoke to us, I almost jumped out of my skin.

"Hello, is anyone there," the woman said sarcastically. She rolled her eyes at us and said, "Are y'all fucking deaf? I said the boss will see you now!"

Slowly getting up from our seats, we began to follow her to a back room that was behind a dirty whitewashed door. Placing her hand on the doorknob, she quickly turned around and yelled, "Tony, could you get these people the fuck out of here." She said this referring to the customers in the laundromat.

"Will do, Lissey," the man at the counter said, getting up from his stool and shooing people out the front door.

"You Sammy?" Lissey asked, looking at me directly in the face.

I nodded my head up and down with an impassive look on my face that caused a little smirk to flash on her face. She shook her head and said, "So young and you're willing to take a life for the girl that you love. Now that's a real man in my opinion."

I could have sworn that after she said that, a tear was getting ready to slide down her left cheek, but she quickly turned her head toward the doorway so as not to let us see her emotions.

Entering the door was like entering the mouth of a demonic beast. My face was quickly assaulted by stank warm air, as if the room itself was breathing. The rhythmic hum of an old boiler seemed to make the room pulsate, as though it had an old heart that was on its last limb. At that moment, I could feel fear gripping my heart, as my eyes began to adjust to the darkness of the room. In front of us was a cinder block wall that was in desperate need of a paint job. The years of dust accumulating on the wall resembled the soot-stained face of a firefighter that just exited a burning building.

"Yo, Lissey, hurry the fuck up and bring those damn kids over here," a watery voice that seemed to be drenched in phlegm growled.

Without responding to the voice that commanded her, Lissey walked around the corner from the entrance with Ace and me following her every step. Rounding the corner of the room, we found Sheila's pops tied to a chair. The man's wrists were bound tightly behind him with dirty yellow rope that seemed to be digging into his flesh. His face was slick with sweat as anxiety took over his body. The motherfucker knew that he was going to die and there was no escaping it. His mouth had been duct-taped to muffle the screams during the preparation for this moment. I could hear the piece of shit plead for his life as I looked into his eyes. Those eyes spoke volumes of forgiveness, but it was too late. He had hurt my love dearly and had to pay.

Under the naked lightbulb in the room, I saw an overweight man with thick gold rope chains around his neck and multiple tattoos on both of his arms. One of those tattoos was of a map of the island of Puerto Rico with fine cursive writing that read, "*Mi Isla Bonita.*"

"Hey, what the fuck, kid? You gonna kill him or you are just gonna stare at me and jerk off all day?" The overweight man growled this with such intensity that it chilled my bones.

"Calm the fuck down, Zepeda. This is his first time doing this," Ace said, coming to my defense.

"Oh, I ain't realize that the little shit was a virgin to this type of thing. Let me tell you something, kid, when you want somebody dead, you kill them without having a second thought. You just say to yourself, 'Hey, that piece of shit just fucked with my well-being,' then you kill the son of a bitch. Now, I know that you know this fact because your Carter's boy and he trained you to be one of the most unstoppable killers on the face of the earth, but it seems to me that you're letting yourself get too caught up in your emotions over this punk-ass's daughter to fulfill your duty at hand." Zepeda chuckled at that notion as he got up from his chair. The gold rope chain around his neck glistened in the light from the naked lightbulb, giving him a strange sort of mystical quality to him that screamed, THIS CAT RUNS SHIT IN THE HOOD!

Making his way toward me, I noticed that Zepeda was carrying a sledgehammer, its smooth jet-black head gleaming in the light as if saying, "I'm ready when you are, little nigga."

Without saying anything else, Zepeda handed me the sledge-hammer and backed away, but before I killed the bastard, I needed to hear why he hurt Sheila. Ripping the duct tape off his mouth, I felt actual glee when he winced in pain.

"Why are you doing this, Sam? I've been nothing but nice to you," Sheila's pops said, as he tried to play the innocent, oblivious victim.

I could feel the anger start to course through my body as I heard this. I took a deep breath before answering. Drool was now dripping from the sides of my mouth, as if I was a rabid dog. "You raped her, Julio!" I screamed, my spit raining down on his face.

As if disregarding the fact that he was going to die, Julio let out a torrent of laughter and said, "Aww, *pobrecito,* I thought you knew she was a little whore," said Julio. At this point, it seemed that he no longer gave a fuck what happened to him. He was just trying to fuck with my emotions for as long as he could. "Yeah, little man, I done popped that bitch's cherry when she was twelve and she liked it, begging for me to—"

Cutting him off midsentence, I swung the sledgehammer as hard as I could, sending the bastard's head clean off his body and smacking into the wall on the left side of the room.

"Holy shit, did you see that? Little dude just went Babe Ruth on that *cabron*," said Zepeda *more* to himself than to the people in the room. Zepeda was so impressed me at that moment that he instantly dubbed me "El Demonio," which means "The Devil" in Spanish. Aside from giving me that moniker, it was that day that he put me on about being a full-time enforcer for his crew.

I can still hear Ace's voice that day as it echoed throughout the streets as we walked home. "You owe me, nigga," Ace kept saying, jumping up and down with excitement. "Yo, do you realize that you are now part of the biggest and baddest crew in Delaware? This is fucking major, baby," he shouted happily as we entered our house.

Making my way up to my room, I found Carter sitting by my window looking out onto the backyard, which was nothing but a solid ground of concrete and a few dead plants. I didn't say a word, but just stood there at the doorway to my room looking at Carter's emaciated form. Heroin had taken its toll on his once robust physique, turning him into a frail old man at age forty-five.

"I know what you did today, Sam," he said as he kept staring out the window. Carter continued to speak. "I talked to Zepeda a few minutes ago over the phone. He said that you are a little wet behind the ears, but that you're a cold-blooded killer. Didn't even flinch when you saw that guy's head flying across the room."

It was at that moment that Carter stopped talking and I just lost all my composure. Tears began to flow down my face as I walked up to him for an embrace. Mind you, not once in my life did Carter hug me, but that day, he hugged me as though he was trying to keep my from withering away in the wind. "It's okay to cry, Sam. It means that you have a heart and still human. Shit, if you didn't cry after your first murder, I would be worried, but that just means that your heart isn't cold. Do you understand what I'm saying?" He said this as he broke our embrace.

That was the first and only time he hugged me. It was then that I knew he loved me like a son. Two weeks later, me and Ace found him dead in bed with a needle stuck in his arm. He had overdosed the night before.

"One love, Pops," I said, as the memory of my first kill and Carter's death relinquished its hold on me, allowing me to step into the late fall of 2017.

CHAPTER SEVEN

"**B**abe, babe, wake up! You gotta come see this," said Sheila. Seeing that I wasn't waking up quick enough, she resorted to hitting me over the head with a pillow. "Babe, wake the fuck up. I got good news," she said, adding more excitement to her already hyped voice.

Wiping the crust away from my eyes, I planted my feet firmly on the floor. Without a word, Sheila handed me a print copy of an email she had received from a publishing company called Hood Renaissance. According to the email, the company had received my manuscript and were hoping to publish it. I couldn't hold back my excitement and happiness. Lifting Sheila off her feet, both of our bodies spun around the room in extreme bliss.

"I have some more good news to tell you," said Sheila, her eyes gleaming with a certain kind of happiness and freedom I had not seen since the day I got rid of her pops.

"What is it?" I asked, feeling overwhelmed.

Tears started to slide down her cheeks as she said, "I'm pregnant, babe."

Overjoyed with this announcement, I kiss her passionately on the lips, but our little moment was interrupted by the ringing of the house phone. I quickly broke away from Sheila's embrace and headed toward the phone because all my instincts told me it was Ace who was calling.

"Nigga, is that you?" Ace's voice sounded as though he was irritated and in a rush.

"Well, hello to you too," I said sarcastically, hoping to lighten Ace up a bit.

"Look, man, we gotta take out Zepeda and his crew now. They're all at a poker game as we speak. We can hit them all now with one swoop and we're done, you feel me?" Ace's logic seemed reckless to me, going in a poker game full of gangsters and shooting them up with no plan whatsoever, but I was sure Ace knew what he was doing, so I was down.

"Yo, I'm outside right now in my car with Uzis in the trunk and a shitload of ammo. It's now or never," said Ace, hanging up the phone.

I ran out the front door without saying anything to Sheila, not even looking back to see the expression on her face. I saw Ace behind the wheel of a beat-up old Lincoln, opened the passenger door, and hopped in. Ace was dressed in a black jumpsuit that made him look like he was going to an audition for the role of Michael Myers in the next *Halloween* flick, complete with white mask and all, which was, at the moment, on his lap as he drove. It didn't take long for me to figure out that he had the same getup for me to wear as well. Without saying a word, I put on the jumpsuit as he drove and placed my Uzi in my lap.

As we made it to the poker game, which was being held in an old first floor apartment near Orange Street, we put on our masks, grabbed our guns, and exited the car, making our way inside the apartment building at full speed like Navy SEALs. Entering the building, we kicked in the door to apartment 1A, letting our Uzis spit round after round at the group of men sitting around a poker table. Things were going so fast that I didn't even see the dudes' faces, but the one face that I saw and was familiar was that of Zepeda, now lying dead on the floor.

Suddenly as we ran back to our car, the thunderous crack of a shotgun sounded behind us, leaving Ace's head into a bloody, pulpy mess. I made it all the way to the driver's side door of the Lincoln when I felt a bullet rip through the left side of my torso. On the real, I thought that that was all she wrote for me, but I knew that it wasn't my time. I could feel it in my heart.

Knowing that I wasn't going to die, my thoughts quickly gathered themselves into an energy that I hadn't felt since I was a teenager, an energy that I only felt during my training with Carter. This energy encompassed my soul, causing me to react as a man possessed. It was as though that shotgun blast that knocked me out awakened something that was dormant in me for years, something that spoke to me in Carter's voice. It was like I was in the middle of one of our training session.

"Get up, nigga! That shotgun blast just grazed you. Move your ass, nigga," Carter's voice yelled throughout my mind, causing me to shrug off the daze that I was in and forcing me to open my eyes to see my would-be killer standing over me as if he was a predator out in the wild examining his prey. The piece of shit must have had something on his mind distracting him because he didn't notice when I picked my Uzi and fired a few shots into his face, causing him to fall to the pavement awkwardly, with his arms flailing like a strange bird.

"Now's your chance nigga, move!" said the voice in my head. Getting up from the pavement, I could see a huge crowd that was gathered across the street gawking at me with their mouths hanging open. It was as though they were witnessing a dead man rising from the grave. At the same time, I could hear the wailing sirens echoing throughout Orange Street. With all the strength that I could muster, I limped into the driver's seat of the Lincoln and found a spare key hidden in the visor above. Starting the ignition, I quickly fishtailed the car onto the road, making the tires screech like a banshee escaping the depth of hell as I sped away from the scene.

My mind kept racing with jumbled thoughts. My mind kept going back to Ace lying dead on the pavement with his head blown off. What the fuck was I going to do now? The at that moment, it was obvious that the Zepeda family already knew that me and Ace were behind that whole fiasco. No doubt that they also knew that I was still alive. Despair suddenly took over me. I felt like a chicken with its damn head cut off, completely lost at that point.

"Man the fuck up, nigga!" Carter's voice yelled in my head. *"Your main priority right now is to get Sheila and get the fuck up out of Dodge. I know you're mourning Ace and want to retaliate, but you need to forget*

about all of that shit and focus on your family right now. Get out of this street life while you still can and forget about seeking vengeance. It's not worth it. Just look at how Ace ended up."

I guess my body was on autopilot because as soon as Carter's voice stopped talking to me, I found myself parked in front of my house, but having no recollection whatsoever of having the desire to head over there. I swear, my mind completely blacked out as soon as I got in the Lincoln and drove off from the scene at Orange Street.

Parking in the middle of the street, I jumped out of the car and ran to the porch. Placing my hand on the knob, my heart sank as I found the door unlocked. Sheila never left the front door unlocked. That was one of her pet peeves. Something was definitely wrong. Opening the door with the force of a hurricane wind, I ran inside like madman screaming Sheila's name at the top of my lungs, only to be greeted with the scene of what seemed to have been a huge struggle. The glass coffee table that sat in the middle of the living room now was shattered into a million pieces. The cream-colored sofa was over-turned, along with the end tables and two busted lamps.

"Sheilaaa!" I yelled at the top of my lungs, as I continued to search all through the house for her, with no success. Making my way to the dining room, I discovered a handwritten letter on the dinner table. It read,

----

Hello there, Sammy,

Why the fuck did you think that you and Ace could pull a fast one on me? I didn't realize that you motherfuckers were so stupid. Jesus, I thought that Carter taught you two better than that? Weren't you two trained in the art of Ninjitsu or some shit like that? If so, then y'all motherfuckers are terrible at it! Anyway, all jokes aside, we've been watching your ass since you got out of prison, so we knew every moved you made. For a while you played the part of a good boy, but you let Ace convince you to fight against us. That was one of your biggest mistakes. You knew as well as I did that Ace was a fucking hothead, so why did you join him on his fool's quest? Come on, Sam, anybody in these streets will tell you that there ain't no loyalty out here, it's every man for himself. That is why I have taken your wife, to toughen you up into a little bitch! Until we meet again.

Tony Zepeda

CHAPTER EIGHT

My entire world seemed to crumble all around me at that moment. Tony Zepeda? I thought that little shit had died years ago. As a matter of fact, I was the one that did the deed. Tony Zepeda was the only son of the head of the Zepeda family. His pops had me take the kid out because he was causing some major beef with the Haitians down in Miami when he wanted to team up with a small Cuban and Puerto Rican crew without his pops knowing anything about it. However, it was by way of the Haitians that his pops found out, after a couple dudes from the crew that Tony wanted to do business with snubbed out a few Haitians. That's when Old Man Zepeda called me in to kill his son.

I remember that shit like it was yesterday. I had been spying on the bastard all week, waiting to see if he made any moves that would do any harm to his pops's business. Tony did meet with a rival Puerto Rican crew that established themselves in an old rundown bodega on Franklin Street. They were nothing, though, just a couple of former stickup kids looking to rise up in the ranks. Aside from that, the dude was pretty boring. When he wasn't chilling with his little bodega crew, he would stay indoors in his townhouse in Greenville having high-price hookers come over. At nights, Tony could be found in the manager's office in a strip club owned by his pops called The King's Lounge. It was there that I decided to make my move. That night I had followed him to the club and made my way to the basement of the club, which could be accessed by two cellar doors behind the building.

As planned by my boss, the cellar doors were left unlocked, granting me easy access without being noticed. Making my way to the office, I could hear Vanity 6's "Nasty Girls" blasting throughout the club. Nobody seem to notice me going up the stairs to the manager's office; they were all entranced by the thick white girl dancing topless onstage. At the top of the stairs, I kicked the door open, interrupting one of the strippers giving head to Tony. She looked up at me like a deer caught in the headlights, and before she could scream, I pulled out my silencer and gave Tony two shots to the dome, splattering his brains all over the wall. For good measure, I shot the stripper he was with between the eyes in case she got any bright ideas to start screaming for help. The hit went off without a hitch (so I thought), and I left the club to report back to the boss.

Now, twenty years later, I stood in my kitchen with a note that seemed to had been written by a ghost. Pondering this notion, I felt a sudden movement behind me, causing me to elbow then roundhouse kick to whatever was behind me. When I felt that it was safe to let my guard down, I saw a dude dressed in black with a ski mask squirming in pain on the kitchen floor. Out of the corner of my eye, I saw the handgun that my attacker used lying a few feet away from him and quickly snatched it up. Pointing the gun at my attacker, I realized that his skills were nowhere near that of a trained assassin, so I let relaxed my guard a bit. "Who sent you?" I asked, kicking the motherfucker in the ribs.

Despite the pain he was feeling, the bastard didn't answer my question, so I kicked him again, this time hearing his ribs crack.

"Tony sent me!" he screamed as if in the form of a submission.

I leaned over him this time and yanked off his ski mask. I wanted to see his face when I asked him my next question, but what was revealed behind that mask was the face of a young boy who couldn't have been no more than sixteen.

"You little shit, how you gonna roll up in my house and try to kill me? Do you know who the fuck you're dealing with, faggot?" I asked the boy as his eyes began to overflow with the fear that was inside of him. It was at that moment that I could feel the darkness that I had repressed for twenty-two years during my incarceration come back full force, with Carter's voice echoing in my mind, saying, *"Welcome back, nigga!"*

With that giving me the strength that I needed, I struck the boy in the face with a gun, causing the boy to bleed from his lower lip. I grabbed the boy by his head and pulled his face up to mine and screamed, "Where the fuck is my wife?!" My voice sounded ferocious, feral, like that of a wild animal growl.

The boy stammered as piss began to form a puddle around him. "S-she's in a...a...w-w-warehouse in Philly," he finally spat out.

"Thanks," I said, putting the barrel of the gun underneath his chin and blasting the little fucker's brains out.

CHAPTER NINE

I t wasn't hard for me to figure out which warehouse the kid was talking about. If there was one thing about the Zepeda family, they were creatures of habit, meaning that if they established themselves in a place, that was where they stayed, and if a rival family tried to attack that place, the Zepeda family would find a way to eliminate them and continue business as usual in the same spot. Sure, it was very high risk to operate in such a fashion, but the Zepeda family were very arrogant folk. Those motherfuckers felt that they couldn't be touched. However, they didn't seem to take into account that they would go up against a dude like me who knew how they operated, and I knew damn well that Tony knew this fact and had big plans for when we met face-to-face. But I had something up my sleeve. I was going to take down all the major Zepeda operations one by one before I saved Sheila, and if Tony was watching me like he said was, I welcomed his goons to come at me.

As I thought this through, the adrenaline in me started to subside, causing me to feel the pain on the side of my body where the shotgun slug had grazed me earlier in the day. Getting some thread and sewing needle from a cabinet upstairs, I headed to the bathroom to clean and sew up my wound using a hand mirror to view my handiwork.

That night, I drove Ace's Lincoln out to Eastside and abandoned it on the side of the road. Exiting the car, I walk to the trunk and banged on it, saying, "Happy trail to you, motherfucker." Laughing out loud, I thought of my attacker, whose corpse was lying stiff and curled up in the trunk. I could feel a little drop of remorse begin to seep into the barricade of darkness that housed my soul once again, as if it was a leaky roof during a heavy rainstorm. But that weak spot was quickly patched up as I convinced myself that the kid asked for it. Shit, I was defending myself. The piece of shit came at me first. With these thoughts flowing through my mind, I thought of Ace. How did he know that old man Zepeda and the main dude that helped run his businesses were going to be at that exact apartment playing poker?

It was then that a lightbulb went off in my head. Right then and there, it became obvious to me that Ace had some kind of dealings with Tony. My blood began to boil with rage as I grappled with the fact that Ace might have hidden the existence of Tony from me. Did Ace plan to fuck me over by teaming up with Tony to take out both his pops and me? Or maybe Tony was using us a pawns to wipe out his pops and his partners and then kill us both after the job was done. I would like to think that the latter was true and not that Ace wanted to set me up, but it was too difficult to say at that time. I didn't know if my thoughts were accurate at the time, but I knew I would find out once I found Tony.

Night was fast approaching as I walked down the road. I was so preoccupied with my thoughts that I had completely forgotten that I was walking down a lonely road on the Eastside, putting myself at risk at getting robbed or jumped by a stickup kid or worse, but I didn't give a fuck. I was on a warpath.

After walking for three hours straight, I came across a small gun shop that had a sign out front that said, "*Welcome to Hank's! American owned and operated since 1972.*" I could almost hear a Southern twang punctuate the words as I read them.

"Ah, just what need right now," I said to myself out loud, bringing the preparation for my mission back into focus. As I walked into the gun shop, the first thing that I saw was a huge Confederate flag hung up high on the wall with words "*This is God's country*" stitched on it. It was then that I knew that I had entered a redneck's gun shop. Its walls were plastered with all kinds of posters that promoted the NRA. Also, there was a wall that was strictly reserved for trophies for big game hunting, which were the heads or bears and tigers, their eyes staring back at me cold and blank.

"Can I help ya there, fella?" said the voice of an old man with a Southern drawl.

I nearly jumped out my fucking skin when I heard that voice. I looked down from the big game trophies and saw an old white dude that was about seventy-nine years old with a neon red baseball cap that read, "*Make America Great Again.*" Aside from the baseball cap, the dude had an extremely long snow-white beard that went almost all the way down to his potbelly, making him look like some kind of a wizard. His plaid shirt and denim overalls smelled of tobacco and mold, as if the dude had been standing in the same spot behind the counter since the store had opened.

"What, are you deaf there, partner?" repeated the old man with a bit of attitude in his voice, snatching my attention from the big game trophies and bringing it back on him.

"Um, yeah, I'm looking for an AK-47 and bullets to go with it," I responded nonchalantly.

The old man gave a little chuckle at my request, as his eyes seem to burn with the bigotry that he held inside. "That's it, just an AK-47 and some bullets? You don't want a brand or model?" He shook his head, sighing deeply. "It figures that a spic like you don't know a god-damn thing about no gun. All you fuckers care about is killin' each other like those damn niggers."

I could feel my rage boiling. I closed my fist and punched the old fuck in the face, sending his head back with a grotesque crack, instantly killing him. With the sound of the body hitting the floor, I took that as my cue to help myself to all the shit that I needed. Seeing that I was the only one in the shop at the time, I quickly turned off the flashing sign that indicated the shop was open and a few lights within the shop.

Observing my surroundings, I notice that the shop was pack with a ton of hunting clothes, everything from combat boots, hunting vests, to a shitload of apparel that was strictly camouflage. Oddly enough, the place even sold long leather jackets, the one that kind of resembled trench coats. Immediately, I started to gather all the things that I needed for what lay ahead, grabbing a long leather jacket as well as a Rambo-style hunting knife, an AK-47, and a ton of bullet clips. A nigga was ready for war, I wasn't playing. As that thought went through my mind, it donned on me that there was most likely a security camera in the shop, which made me focus my attention on looking for some sort of a room that a security system might be installed in. My eyes soon landed on a door behind the counter that read, "Employees Only."

"Jackpot," I said, jumping over the counter and breaking open the lock on the door. Opening the door, I saw what looked to be an old closed-circuit TV with a VCR whizzing a VHS tape inside of it. The TV monitor displayed a black-and-white top-down view of the shop. I quickly ejected the tape and stomped the shit out of it, destroying the damn thing as best I could. After disposing of the tape, it didn't take long for me to realize that the room that the room I was standing in housed a plethora of guns, grenades, and explosives. "Fuck, I actually did this country a favor by killing that piece of shit. It looks like he was preparing for a war or some shit," I said out loud, remembering the neo-Nazi fucks in prison jabbering on about how there was going to by a race war in America between blacks and whites. Well, I guess those white boys were now down one soldier.

Taking a few grenades and six bombs and putting them in a large duffel bag that I found in the shop, I walked out the back door, which led out to a small garage that house an old white van that had no side windows on its back half. The van itself reminded me of the kind that pedophiles used to kidnap kids.

"This must be my lucky day," I said, as I found what seemed to be an extra set of keys to the van hanging from a peg by the door, but before I drove away in it that ancient monstrosity, I needed to check it out first. Opening the van's rear doors, I discovered that there was an old army cot with a pillow and a thin blue sheet, provoking sleepiness and fatigue to take over my body. The toll of the day's events had finally taken over my body. I figured that with a rest, I could better formulate a plan to take down the Zepeda family.

As soon as my body fell on that cot, I was out like a light. I dreamt of Sheila that night. That particular dream that night consisted of a memory of our first date. It had been two weeks after the poetry reading where I had gotten her attention. We had agreed to meet at Banning Park at dusk. Sheila had come equipped with a small AM/FM radio and a beach blanket with Bart Simpson embossed on it with a word bubble that read, *"Don't Have A Cow, Man."* We found a nice quiet spot on a grassy knoll where Sheila laid out her beach blanket and turned on her radio, tuning the dial to Power 99 FM. As she messed with the radio's dial, my eyes were glued to the sky. Dusk had now turned into night, allowing me to see what seemed to be a kingdom of stars for the first time in my life. On the real, it was so beautiful that I almost cried, but was sidetracked by romantic thought that I decided to share with Sheila. "Yo, Sheila, you ever wonder if the stars confuse us for their gods?"

She looked at me as a slight giggle escaped her mouth. "Nigga, do you ever turn that poetic shit off," she said jokingly as she kissed my lips.

As if on cue, "Pretty Brown Eyes" by Mint Condition began to play softly on the radio. The soft sweet melody of the song had us in a trance, causing us to get up and slow dance.

"I love you, Sammy," whispered Sheila in my ear.

That's when I pulled back to look into her eyes and discovered that her face had melted down to her skull, as she screamed, "Wake the fuck up, nigga!" These words were said in a demonic voice, jolting me from my sleep, all drenched in sweat and trying to catch my breath.

A plan finally came to me. I was going to take down Zepeda's four main trap houses in the city and the one he had down in Florida as well. Those four trap houses were the spine of the family's entire operation. Taking those houses out would cripple them for good. Those motherfuckers were surely going to feel my wrath. I could feel my blood boiling in anticipation as I got into the front seat of the van and headed to the first trap house on West Fourth Street.

Parking three blocks from my intended target, I donned the long leather coat that I nabbed from the gun shop, stuffing one of the small bombs in one of the inner pockets of the coat. I ain't gonna lie, the weight of the small bomb in my pocket made me feel like I was invincible. It was as though the bomb itself created a strange force field around me that emanated pure death to anybody that tried to take my life. This feeling was so strong that instead of taking a gun with me, I chose the damn hunting knife. Exiting the van, I put my hood up over my head and started to walk like a junkie that was aching to get a fix. Dragging my feet along the pavement while scratching my arms, I could feel the cool breath of the dawn encompass my body. It was as though the darkness of predawn was clinging as a way to survive the oncoming daylight.

Walking past the row homes on West Fourth, I could feel my old ways coming back to me, as if a demon was awakened from its slumber, ready to play. I could feel it flexing its muscles and getting its blood coursing through its numb limbs, ready to stalk and kill its prey. Making my way closer to the trap house, I noticed that one of Tony's lackeys was sitting on the front stoop with plastic white earbuds plugged into his ears. His eyes seemed to be glazed over by a memory that was probably conjured up by whatever he was listening to. Hoping that the kid's distraction would buy me some time to sneak up behind him and slit his throat, I hid in the shadows that were provided by a few parked cars beside the curb. Slowly taking out my hunting knife, I saw no need to walk pretend that I was a junkie when I could just sneak up behind the fucker and take him out. However, if this was back in the day, though, I would have had to play the part of a junkie because the cats that Zepeda had working for him were like night owls, alert as shit. Hell, it didn't matter to none, I was right at home in the shadows, letting them embrace me like old friends at a "welcome back" party.

I stayed laid up against a parked that was directly under a busted streetlamp, giving me the perfect cover as I waited for the piece of shit to turn his back toward me so that I could make my move. With his hands tucked into his dark Sean John coat, the dude got up from the stoop and turned to go in the house. Thanks to the music that blasted through his earbuds, I didn't have to conceal the sounds of my footsteps on the pavement, allowing me to move quicker. Sneaking up behind the bastard, I slashed his throat without hesitation, his thick dark blood cascading from the wound onto the front of his coat. The poor fuck didn't even know what hit him. Before the corpse could hit the ground, I hoisted it up over my shoulder like a sack of potatoes and carried him inside. The dude's earbuds had fallen out, dangling at the sides of his face, which granted me the chance to hear what he was listening to when I killed him. *"When I die bury me inside the Gucci store. All I want for my birthday is a big booty hoe!"*

I ain't even gonna front, I felt like laughing my ass off when I heard the shit that cat was listening to when he died. "Well, it looks like I did you a favor, kid. Shit, anybody who is a fan of shitty rap like that needs to be put out of their misery," I mumbled softly, putting the body down in a living room that was filled with crackheads and heroin addicts who were too high to care that I'd put a dead body among them.

The smell of piss, shit, and vomit assaulted my nose as I proceeded to the second floor of the house, tiptoeing up the stairs with bloody knife in hand. The sound of Jodeci's hit song "Feenin'" floated softly down the stairs, which gave me the indication that there was at least one person on the second floor. This prompted me to be hyper-vigilant of my surroundings.

"Careful, nigga, there could be a motherfucker waiting to slit your throat at the top of those stairs," cautioned the voice of Carter in my head.

Making my way to the top of the stairs, I have to say that I was kind of disappointed to discover that there was no one ready to attack me. Lord knows that my ass was prepared for anything at that point. Instead, when I made it to the landing on the second floor, I came upon a dimly lit hallway that smelled of blueberry-scented candles that came from an open bedroom door where the sounds of Jodeci emanated from. Pressing my body against the wall next to the open doorway, I could hear the passionate groans of a Spanish broad getting dicked-down *"Aye, asi. Damelo duro, cabron!"* the chick groaned in her Puerto Rican dialect.

Taking a peek into the room, I noticed that it was pitch black, save for a stream of light that came from the hallway. From what I could see, a dude was pounding the broad's shit like there was no tomorrow. Seeing that the chick's eyes were closed and her man's back was turned toward the door, I tiptoed in the room and slashed the dude's throat while he was in midhump. His body slid off the chick, falling sideways off the bed as he clutched his bloody throat, hopelessly trying to stop the massive hemorrhaging. The broad the dude was fucking let out a high-pitched scream when she realized what was going on, but that was no bother. I simply grabbed her by the face and rammed her head into the headboard with all my strength, hearing a satisfying crack as I crushed the back of her skull.

As I made my way out the room, my attention was captured by the vibrating sound of a cell phone. Curious, I made my way toward the nightstand and picked up the phone, reading the text message that was just left. "*The hit on Don Goldman is a go for tonight. The bitch is already at his crib. That lawyer faggot is going to regret ever crossing us*," it read.

My heart went into my throat after reading that text. What kind of shit did Goldman have going on with the Zepeda crew, I wondered. Whatever it may have been, I needed to warn his ass pronto.

CHAPTER TEN

"*A* *re you retarded, nigga? That damn fool is as good as dead. Focus on your own shit!*" The voice of Carter was yelling wildly in my head as I ran down to the basement of the house to duct-tape the small bomb that was in my coat to a pillar. Luckily, I knew for a fact that that house in particular didn't have workers packaging the drugs in the basements of other homes, which meant it would be easier to set the bomb with no problem. Making my way down the creaky wooden steps, I saw stacks upon stacks of crack cocaine and heroin along a wall, almost as though the entire stack was a makeshift pillar holding up the house.

"Damn, all this product here and so carelessly guarded," I said out loud, in an attempt to block out Carter's voice from my mind. I guess that's the way things were with the Zepeda family. Hell, I ain't gonna front, if I was the head of a crew that monopolized the entire drug game in Delaware, I would be kind of careless too.

After duct-taping the bomb to a pillar that was set in the middle of the basement, setting its timer to go off in five minutes, I ran back up to the living room to see if I could steal a cell phone off one of the addicts that were stoned out their minds. Luckily, it only took a couple seconds to dig into an addict's pockets and come away with an old-school flip phone. Exiting the house, I could honestly say that at that particular moment I felt no remorse for what happened to those addicts when the house blew up. Shit, as far as I was concerned, I was doing society a favor. Plus, they just happen to be in the wrong place at the wrong time.

The sun had risen as I walked back to the van. Jumping into the driver's seat and closing the door, a monstrous boom sounded throughout the block, as it shook the ground beneath me. I couldn't help but smile as I drove. People were running out of their homes scared shitless over what they heard and just felt. Hell, some of those poor souls must have thought that the end of the world was upon them, or that some crazy dragon was wreaking havoc in the ghetto. Little did they know that it a just an old-ass Puerto Rican trying to save the life of his girl and getting his revenge.

Driving away slowly so as not to hit the people that were running wildly in the street, I dug into my pants pocket and took the flip phone that I had nabbed and dialed Goldman's number. To my relief, he picked up on the first ring.

"Who the fuck is this?!" yelled Goldman on his end, sounding like he was gasping for air.

At that moment, I didn't care what the hell he was doing, I just wanted him out of harm's way. "Listen to me, Donald," I said in a grim and serious tone without any type of greeting whatsoever. "I need you to listen to me very carefully, man. The Zepeda family has a hit put out on you." On the real, when I broke that news to him, I thought his ass would have been shocked and scared shitless.

Instead, Goldman sounded gangster, saying, "Yeah, no shit, man. I just iced my so-called assassin a few minutes ago." At first, I thought he was being sarcastic, but as soon as I realized that he was trying to catch his breath without making a smart-ass joke, I knew he was serious.

Without me asking Goldman for details of how everything went down, he began to give them to me rapidly, as if his mouth was a machine gun spitting round after round. "Dude, I was fucking this fine Latin babe She was riding my dick like a good ole cowgirl. Suddenly, while I'm all up in the pussy, the bitch decided to pull a knife out of nowhere. Luckily, my ass got quick reflexes, and I tagged her in the face, causing the bitch to fall to the floor. Seeing that she was dazed from the blow to the face that I'd just given her, I got on top of her with all my weight and started to bang her head on my hardwood floor until she stopped squirming and her head was in a puddle of blood."

By the time Goldman finished his story, I could tell that he was shook.

I sighed as I tried to figure out why Tony Zepeda would put a hit out on Goldman. What had he gotten himself into? I had to know the answer. Shit, that hit could have had something to do with me. Maybe Goldman knew something that I didn't. I cleaned my throat and began to speak. "Where you at now, Donald?"

There was silence on the other end of the phone, showing me that there were trust issues floating around in Goldman's mind. I let the silence draw out for at least two minutes before I said, "I'm trying to help you, Don. I am not working for Zepeda anymore. The piece of shit has been fucking me over for years. Anyway, Ismael Zepeda is dead now, but now his son Tony is in charge of the entire operation." I could sense the relief in Goldman as the sound of a deep sigh broke the silence on the other end of the phone.

"Who killed the bastard?"

I couldn't help but sense the optimism creeping into his voice as he asked that question. Confident that the phone I was on wasn't tapped by law enforcement or the Zepeda crew, I nonchalantly stated that I had killed Ismael.

There was a slight pause on the other end before Goldman answered. I could feel the tension growing as the minute of silence seemed to stretch out into eternity. "You did what now?" The alarm in Goldman's voice flew into hysterics, as if he was on the edge of insanity. "Hold on, let's backtrack a bit," said Goldman, taking deep shallow breaths as if he was hyperventilating. "You killed Zepeda because he fucked you over?" Judging from the tone of his voice, I could tell that he didn't believe me, causing me to sigh in frustration.

"Look, man, where the hell are you?" I asked that question, letting it ride the wave of my annoyance.

"All right, dude, chill," said Goldman, with fear drowning his every word. "I'm holed up at Luck's Motel right off the Jersey turnpike." After he said this, I could sense a deep regret in his voice, which awoke suspicion right away. I knew right then that the moth-erfucker was planning to kill me.

I must have been out of my mind going to meet up with a dude that I thought was going to kill me. I had to seek him out on the off chance that he was just scared and needed protection. Aside from that fact, I realized that I needed help on my mission. There was no way in hell I could take down Zepeda empire on my own. Shit, not with that bomb I set off in that trap house. At that very moment, I knew that the Zepeda family were doubling up on their manpower, and I was too fucking old for that one-man army Rambo shit. The way I saw it, maybe Goldman knew somebody that would be willing to help me out—that is, if I could prevent him from killing me first.

CHAPTER ELEVEN

Entering New Jersey, the first thing that caught my eye was a huge sign that was shaped like a giant domino piece that boldly displayed "Lucky's" in bold fancy letters like it was the name of some five-star hotel. Sadly, however, that wasn't the case. The building that sign advertised was nothing more than a clapboard piece of shit that boasted eight rooms and a gravel parking lot that only had two cars parked in it, Goldman's Benz and what I assumed to be the motel owner's navy blue Ford pickup truck. The gravel in the parking lot crunched underneath the tires of the van, alerting those inside the motel that someone had arrived. I figured that Goldman now knew that I was here for sure. I could picture him next to a window standing behind a curtain yellowed with age with a semiautomatic rifle cocked like Malcolm X daring someone to attack.

Approaching Goldman's room at the end of the motel, I could sense that someone was following me, but I played it cool and went about my business. Jesus, Tony must have forgotten who he was messing with. I should have felt insulted, but instead felt elated at the fact that the predictability of Tony's crew would make it easier for me to kill. I just wished that I had been carrying a sniper rifle with me at that moment so I could pick off the fucker that was following me without giving him a chance to attack. It would have been less messy, in my opinion, and a hell of a lot quicker too, but what's done is done.

I knocked on Goldman's hotel door, expecting him to open it right away pointing a gun at me, but I was greeted with what seemed to be a set of muffled voices on the other side of the door.

"See, I knew that lawyer bastard was gonna light you up, but you just had to come and save his ass. Nigga, did you ever pay attention to what I taught you? Now they're gonna light your dumb ass up," scolded the voice of Carter, as I jumped out the way of the way of the machine gun rounds that were piercing through the door from the inside of the room. At that moment, shots also rang out from behind me, causing me to take cover behind a pillar that held up an awning that spanned the length of the entire motel. From the corner of my eye, I could see the fucker that shot at me from behind as he sped away in rusted white car from the 1950s. Before the bastard could get away, I quickly dug out my pistol from one of the pockets of my leather coat and fired at the driver, watching the bullet enter the side of his head. The dude was killed instantly, causing the car to swerve into the navy blue pickup truck. All this seemed to happen in a matter of seconds as the door to Goldman's room opened and two men dressed in black came at me guns blazing, but before any of their bullet could whiz in my direction, I jumped high into the air and drop-kicked him in the throat. The guy was dead before he hit the ground.

Seeing that the target he was trying to destroy just murdered his boy with a single kick to the throat, the second gunman became frozen with fear, which somehow seemed to paralyze the motherfucker's trigger finger. Within that small window of cease fire, I grabbed the bastard's neck and snapped it like a twig. As the dude's body fell limp to the ground, I quickly made my way inside Goldman's motel room.

Upon entering, my sense of smell was assaulted by the pungent scent of shit and vomit, a grotesque mixture that indicated that someone was tortured before being disposed of. I feared the worst for Goldman. I could feel anxiety coursing through my veins as my eyes searched the entire room, to no avail; Goldman was nowhere to be found. The room was in complete shambles. An end table that would have normally been beside the bed looked like it had been thrown across the room, smashed against the wall that faced the foot of the bed. A black leather-bound Bible was sticking out of its open draw, grotesquely looking like a thick tongue, making the end table resemble the carcass of a dead animal that lay on its side. The mattress on the twin bed was stained with blood in various places. Some of the stains were fresh while others had begun to brown and orange with time gone by. The mattress itself was slightly askew on the bed, revealing the skeletal frame of the box spring Even the walls above had splotches of dried blood on them. Yup, Goldman had definitely put up a fight, but where the fuck was he? I had a gut feeling that he wasn't dead. For God's sake, I had spoken to him thirty minutes prior. I knew that was faulty logic, but I had to cling on to something. That's when it donned on me to call his cell phone. To my surprise, I could hear the standard xylophone ringtone of Goldman's iPhone going off in the bathroom. I quickly made my way there with hope beginning to wash over me.

"Please, God, let Don be alive," I caught myself reciting in a mantra as I opened the door. Letting Goldman's phone ring until its voice mail picked up, I reached into the darkened bathroom and flicked on the light before stepping in, revealing a hog-tied Goldman looking up at me from a mustard yellow bathtub with disparity in his eyes.

Noticing my presence, Goldman began to squirm, begging me to untie him, his disparity seemed to build up with every groan and mumble that was barricaded by the duct tape covering his mouth. With pity and relief washing over me, I removed the duct tape with one quick tug.

"Fuuuck! Dude, did you have to do that so hard," whined Goldman as I began to untie him. As I did so, he began to talk nervously in rapid succession, as though a pipe full of emotions had burst inside of him. "Man, I thought I was a goner for sure. When those two Spanish guys came knock at the door, I thought that it was you, so I opened it without checking who it was first. The next thing I know, those two bastards stormed in, tied me to the bed, and tortured me, removing my toenails with pliers and cutting me with a glowing hot straight razor, removing chunks of my flesh."

I don't know why Goldman was telling me all this when I could clearly see what those bastards had done to him with my own eyes, but I think he was talking because the sound of his own voice assured him that he was alive.

"Dude, I don't know what the fuck you did to get yourself into mess, but you're gonna have to tell me everything," I said as I untied his hands and feet. "Do you think you can walk on your own?" I asked, pulling him up on his feet, to no avail. "Fuck it, I'll carry you," I said, swooping Goldman over my shoulder like a sack of potatoes and making my way out of the motel room.

Making my way out the door, I heard rapid footsteps approaching, which made me quickly take out my pistol, pointing it at the doorway. As the owner of the running footsteps appeared, I didn't even give him a chance to pass the threshold before I blasted him. With the dude's head lying in a pulpy heap of his brains, I realized that he must have been the proprietor of the motel. With his shotgun lying forlornly beside his outstretched hands and his plaid shirt drenched in blood, it was obvious that the dude was only trying to defend his joint from the chaos that was happening. I shook my head in pity and walked over the dude's body, crossing over the graveled parking lot, which now resembled a warzone in Iraq.

When I made it to the van, I plopped Goldman in the passenger seat and made my way to the back of the van to search for one of those bombs. Finding one, I shut the back door to the van and made my way over to Goldman's Benz, smashing the driver's side door in and opening the door to set the bomb on the dashboard. After setting up the bomb in Goldman's car, I made sure to grab all the shit that was in his glove compartment—license, registration, anything that could lead back to Goldman being there. Shit, I even took the damn license plate off for good measure and hauled ass back to the van.

As I hopped in the driver's seat, an earsplitting thunderclap shook the earth the van, causing me to look through my rearview at the Benz and the motel office that was engulfed in flames. Shit, thank God Goldman parked his car so close to the registration office. With any luck, the flames would consume the entire motel, leaving no evidence that we were ever there. Sirens started to wail in the distance, with the moaning of death echoing throughout the atmosphere as Goldman and me sped down the highway two miles away.

CHAPTER TWELVE

"You better start talking, motherfucker. I just risked my life for you," I said, letting my anger get the best of me. Goldman looked at me like a deer caught in the headlights and then went on staring out the windshield in silence. I could feel the rage start to boil in the pit of my stomach, as if it were a caldron bubbling over and spilling into my soul. Screeching to a halt on the side of the road, I pulled out my pistol and pointed its barrel underneath Goldman's jaw and growled, "Look, motherfucker, you better tell me what of kind shit you had going on with the Zepeda family before I finish the job those two faggots back there couldn't do."

With terror overshadowing his face like a storm cloud over the sun, Goldman began to speak in heavy stutter. "I, um…was laundering m-money f-f-for Tony a-and decided t-t-to take a little off the top f-for m-m-myself." Goldman said this as if his mouth were constipated and his vocal cords had trouble pushing sound out to make words.

Without giving it much thought, I took my pistol and whipped him across the face with it, splitting open his lips, instantly turning his mouth into a bloody maw. "You stupid fuck! What, did you think you were in a fucking movie?" I yell in face, trying to avoid looking at the pitiful mask of fear that encompassed his face. "Jesus, you stupid fuck. You gave Tony information about me, didn't you?" I said as the weight of that realization started sinking in the right places like Tetris blocks.

Suddenly all the love I had for Goldman was swallowed by a tide of anger and hatred as I realized that he was in on Sheila's kidnapping. I could feel every fiber in my being holding me back from busting two shots in Goldman's dome. *"Don't do it, nigga, you need that piece of shit right now,"* admonished Carter's voice, cooling down my anger some.

As if reading my mind, Goldman started to speak rapidly, as if trying to get everything off his chest at once. "Look, man, it wasn't my fault. They threatened me and the well-being of my family. One of those motherfuckers is even dating my mom down in Florida, so if I fuck up, they'll kill her. You gotta understand that I couldn't let happen. I love my mom, man," Goldman whined like a frightened little boy. His eyes began welling up with tears as remorse started to bare its weight on his conscience, but the rage that bubbled inside me showed no pity for him and drove me to pistol-whip him again.

"When did Tony first approach you about laundering his money?" I asked this calmly, as though we were two homies kicking it on the back porch and not two dudes caught in a life-or-death situation.

"The deal went down two months before you got out of prison," said Goldman in a matter-of-fact tone, as he wiped the blood from his mouth. "Look, man, after the laundering deal went down, Tony and his fucking goons came back to my office the next day and started asking mad questions about you. They wanted to know if you had family living in or around Delaware. They also wanted to know where you would be staying upon your release from prison. When I didn't divulge this information, that's when they threatened my family, showing me pictures of my mom out having dinner with her new boyfriend at a restaurant. Jesus, Sammy, understand that I had no fucking choice. I had to protect my family."

With Goldman's words digging into my soul like sharpened daggers, I raised my pistol, pressing it to his forehead, and asked through gritted teeth, "What about my family, motherfucker? You put Sheila in danger. You let them know my every move. You're lucky I need your ass right now. Otherwise, I would've lit your ass up by now."

Goldman went cross-eyed as he looked at the barrel of the pistol pressed against his forehead.

"But you're lucky, you know why? Because as fucked up as it seems, you're the only one that I can trust right now."

Before responding, Goldman took a deep breath, as if swallowing a huge of fear. "What do you want me to do?" he asked, sounding like a little boy that was just about to get hazed by a school bully. I lowered the pistol from his forehead, hoping to alleviate some of the stress that I'd created for him so that he could talk and think more confidently. "I know that you are aware of motherfuckers that want to take down Tony as much as do. I also know that you have worked as an attorney for some of those cats."

Goldman's eyes began to light up as if the person that came to his mind suddenly flicked a switch in his brain.

"Of course, how could I forget him," said Goldman, as if talking to himself. He looked up at me with a fresh glow of determination beaming from his face, as if the beating he suffered from Tony's goons never happened. He cleared his throat and started to speak. "In 2006, I defended this cat named Andre Austin, a veteran of the Iraq War. Serving in the military, he was given the nickname Pyro for his expertise in explosives. Anyway, long story short, he was captured and tortured by an insurgence group, which left the poor bastard literally half crazy. Fuck, he was so crazy that he murdered the entire rescue team that saved his ass. He even chopped some of those dudes into little pieces. Pyro was court-martialed for that shit, but I helped him escape the death penalty by copping an insanity plea. He spent five years in an asylum until his escape in 2011, when he found out that his wife and kids were murdered by the Zepeda family, so if anyone has an ax to grind with Tony, it's Pyro."

Letting all that sink in, I couldn't stop the next question from coming out of my mouth. And I hated how desperate and hopeless I sounded. "Do you know where they're keeping Sheila, Don?"

He nodded solemnly with a grave look on his face. "When those two assholes had me tied up in the bathroom of my motel room, I overheard them saying that Sheila was being held captive in a warehouse somewhere in Philadelphia, but they moved her to some sort of compound down in Florida." The words were coming out of Goldman's mouth a mile a minute, as though he was afraid that he wouldn't get them out in time before I broke his jaw.

"Is there any chance that this Pyro dude can help me find her?" I asked, hoping against hope.

At the sound of my question, Goldman's face lit up like a Christmas tree. "There's only one way to find out." Goldman grabbed his phone and began to tap wildly on the screen, sending Pyro a text message. "We're in!" he said gleefully after sending the text. "He wants to meet with us as soon as possible."

CHAPTER THIRTEEN

Twilight was creeping on the edge of the horizon as we approached Pyro's hideout. According to Goldman, he was the one that helped Pyro go into hiding when he escaped the asylum, providing him with an apartment that was located below a run-down liquor store that he owned.

"Why are you helping the guy and putting yourself at risk?" I asked, letting curiosity wash over me.

"I just felt sorry for the dude, sue me." Goldman shrugged, as if helping out escaped mental patients was an everyday occurrence for him. "Park right here, dude," said Goldman as a dilapidated three-floored building came into view on the left side of the road.

The building's faded pink siding was peeling around the edges, revealing how rotted the structure was. A flashing blue and red "Open" sign blinked in its window, as if letting the world know that it was still alive and kicking. With a squealing of its brakes, I parked the van on the curb and got out to assist Goldman out of the passenger seat. Careful not to touch any of Goldman's wounds, I set him down feet first on the pavement, letting him gather his bearings.

"This way," Goldman said, directing me toward a narrow set of stairs that led down to Pyro's apartment, its door a faded whitewash that was peeling off and revealing splinters of aging wood. From the scuffed rectangular window beside the door emanated a soft warm glow of light as loud hip-hop music vibrated through the window-pane. "Well, at least we know that he's home," said Goldman with a nervous little laugh.

Knocking at the door, Goldman began to tense up, as if he were an animal in the wild that could sense danger.

"Damn, dude! Will you calm the fuck down? I thought this Pyro cat was your man and shit. Your ass is acting like we about to meet the devil himself," I said, trying to hold back laughter that was about to bust out my chest.

Goldman looked down at his feet as though he was ashamed. "Sam, you don't know Pyro like I do. That man's a one-man army. He wiped out an entire platoon by himself."

I could see the fear flooding into Goldman's eyes as he said this, and I had to stifle a laugh that crawled from the depths of my gut and desperately wanted to escape from the back of my throat. "You make this cat sound like a superhero or some shit," I said with a little bit of a giggle finally releasing into the atmosphere.

"Shit, laugh all you want, but Pyro was riddled with bullet holes when they found his ass wandering the streets of Baghdad. Shit, I'm talking some real *Luke Cage* shit. When they asked the motherfucker what he thought kept him alive, he told them revenge was the reason."

As Goldman was finishing up his story, the door to the apartment swung open, revealing a tall husky black man with thick black frames on his scarred face and a black-and-white Yankees fitted cap atop his head. His crisp white tee hung loosely off his body as if he had lost a tremendous amount of weight. Looking at the dude's face, he was a dead ringer for K'wan, the urban crime novelist.

"Damn, nigga, what the fuck happened to you?" asked Pyro, directing his question to Goldman as we walked in.

"I had a little run-in with Zepeda's goons," Goldman said sheepishly.

"Shit, I'll say! It looks like you got hit by a fucking Mack truck, then you got attacked by a rabid wolf," said Pyro, examining Goldman from head to toe. "Dude, you better let me take a look at you real quick," said Pyro, his voice filled with fatherly concern, nothing at all like what I expected a crazed soldier's voice to be. Pyro took hold of Goldman and help him walk to a beat-up blue armchair that had yellow stuffing protruding from the arms and side.

As Goldman sat down, he stripped down to his boxer shorts, revealing a heavy amount of bruising around his torso and also the two large gashes where the bastards took out chunks of flesh. Despite how bad he looked, Goldman's eyes emanated a sense of peace, as if he was finally at home. On the real, though, I thought that motherfucker was going to die in that damn armchair.

Meanwhile, Pyro busied himself around the small apartment, gathering the essentials needed to tend to Goldman's wounds. On the real, I was kind of shocked at how that dude was acting toward Goldman. Nowhere was there a trace of the war-torn monster that Goldman described minutes earlier. As a matter of fact, I even doubted that this dude could go up against Tony and his goons—that is, until my eyes swept the entire living room, if I could call it that.

To say that Pyro had had a living room was somewhat of a lie because the room that I was standing in at that moment was nothing short of a war room/science lab. As I walked about the room, I could see all kinds of maps posted high above the battered steel work benches that ran the length of the walls on either side. Posted on the maps themselves were pictures of high-ranking members of the Zepeda family, all of whom I knew personally. Hell, even my picture was posted on one of those maps, except where there was once written the word "Enforcer" was a huge line drawn through it and the words "Pyro's Ally" written beside it. I could see right then and there that Pyro's vendetta with the Zepeda family ran deeper than mine. Shit, this dude knew where every member of the family rested their heads. This was indicated by the pinpoints he had tacked up on every street on the maps. Then the question hit me like a ton of bricks. If this dude knew where everybody rested their heads, why didn't he just snuff them and get it over with?

"What's going on, B? You like my map?" Pyro's voice boomed from behind me, almost making me shit myself. "My bad, man, I didn't mean to scare you," Pyro said sarcastically. His scarred face split into a grotesque smile that seemed to take up the entire bottom half of his face, as if to say, "*I know what you were thinking, nigga. I am going to kill all those fools, but you got exempt. This is your lucky day!*"

The awkwardness of the moment seemed to smother me, as I couldn't decide whether trust the dude or not. I mean, I *was* on a list of men that were going to be killed by this man. I cleared my throat, as if the mere sound of me removing phlegm from my throat shattered the wall of awkward silence and help catapult my question. "I don't get it, if you know where all these fuckers rest their heads, why don't you light them all up and get it over with?"

Pyro roared with laughter, as if the sound of my question was tickling him to the core of his soul. "Aww, man, you don't get it, do you? One doesn't kill for the sake of revenge. No, killing a motherfucker is an art form. It takes time. You see, every motherfucker on this planet is born to be a killer. It's in our DNA, you know. It is a natural tool that God gave man for our survival. We need those in our DNA to capture our prey. To sit back in the shadows and observe every minute detail of their actions until you catch your prey in their most vulnerable moment, then you pounce on the fucker with full force." Pyro finished his speech with a demon-like gleam in his eye, as if he were keeping something from me. He looked at me like he had finally obtained what he wanted for so very long. On the real, the dude freaked me the fuck out. Pyro cleared his throat and continued with what he was saying. "You see, once you discover your prey's vulnerability, you become an artist because now you come up with a way to subdue your prey and survive. Remember, survival is an art unto itself."

Pyro then grabbed a rectangular object that had a glossy screen the size of a hardback book. He turned it on and gave his full attention to the screen. "Oh, shit nigga, this you!" Pyro said gleefully, turning the screen toward me. To my surprise, the screen displayed a black-and-white picture of me from the nineties, standing on the corner of Lancaster and Harrison with my hands in my pockets. Alongside the photo was the cover of my book, *Confessions of a Hit Man.* The cover itself displayed a man's silhouette with his back against the wall, his gun cocked at his side as he stared out the window.

Sheila would have love to see that, I thought to myself as my heart started to scream out in pain for the first time since the shit hit the day before. My eyes started to well up with tears that I so desperately wanted to hold back but couldn't. I was swept away by the wild currents of my emotions, literally falling to my knees. I wept shamelessly in front of Pyro. The force of my sobs making my chest heave as a primal guttural sound escaped the back of my throat.

Pyro stared at me impassively, as if watching a cold-blooded murderer break down in tears was an everyday occurrence for him. After a few seconds, Pyro took a couple of steps toward me and helped to my feet. "Holy fuck," he said, mesmerized. "I've never seen such a beautiful demon in my life."

I looked at him like he had lost his mind. I could feel my old homophobic feelings creeping into my heart and was ashamed.

As if reading my mind, Pyro said, "Not like that, nigga! What I mean is that you have love in your heart. If you were a *real* demon, you wouldn't have broken down into tears just now. Real demons don't have emotion. We entertain ourselves by subduing our prey and creating our art. But you, you are different. There is a great deal of love in your heart, I can feel that. Man, I can tell that being a killer is not in your blood. You were taught to be one. Or maybe there was somebody who taught you how to be human. Whatever the case, I know what will help shed that demon flesh right off of you. Peep this out real quick," said Pyro, walking toward an open doorway that had a blueish glow emanating from it. As I followed Pyro into the room. I couldn't help but feel vulnerable and weak for letting him see me so exposed like that. According to Carter's teachings, me blubbering on the floor was the ultimate sign of my weakness, which would give Pyro an opening to kill me. However, something deep down inside me suggested that I trust him.

As we made our way into the room, I was greeted by a huge bank of closed-circuit TVs that took up an entire wall of the room. "You see this shit right here, homey?" asked Pyro, gesturing toward the TVs. "These are my eyes and ears to the Zepeda's organization." He said this in a proud manner, stretching out his arms wide as if showing off a work of art displayed on the wall.

Below the bank of closed-circuit TVs was a strange panel that displayed what seemed like a million buttons. Shit, if I didn't know any better, I would have guess that the room that I was standing in was some kind of situation room found at a government agency. Each TV screen displayed a different room in a giant facility that I wasn't familiar with.

As if already knowing that I didn't know what those TVs were monitoring, Pyro looked at me and said, "It looks to me that the Zepeda crew kept you in the dark about a lot of things." A dry smile cracked his face once again, as if saying, "You poor ignorant fuck, you didn't know that you were just a worthless pawn."

Shaking his head as if to get rid of that thought, Pyro began to explain what we were looking at on the bank of monitors. "What you're looking at right now is Tony's new drug facility that is located on a huge twenty-acre farm in Dover, Delaware."

Shit, if I didn't know any better, I'd swore that Pyro sounded like a real estate agent that was trying to sell me a piece of property.

He cleared his throat as he started to speak. "On this farm, Tony is able to produce all the cocaine and heroin his heart desires, cutting out the main supplier. In other words, Tony doesn't have to worry about getting his product overseas. Nope, he is now his own supplier. That nigga is sitting pretty, if you ask me," said Pyro, pressing various buttons on the console to make one of the images on one of the TVs take up the entire bank.

"I know what you're thinking," Pyro states with a huge smile on his face. "How the fuck can that nigga grow his own coke and heroin in a place like Delaware? This bum-fuck of a state doesn't have the climate for that shit." He taps a key on the console, changing the image on the TVs to one of a factory that housed massive steel machines that were attached to at least three conveyor belts that were chugging out package after package of cocaine and heroin.

"All of the shit you see there is synthetic. Not a single plant in nature had anything to do with it," said Pyro, his voice drenched in awe. "The thing is, I have no fucking idea what substances or materials Tony is using to fabricate the drugs. Another crazy thing about this entire operation is that the drugs that are made in this factory have the same effect on a junkie as do the real thing. It's hard to tell the difference. I tried it out for myself," he said nonchalantly, as if though he was confirming the great taste of a vintage wine.

Before Pyro got back to the topic at hand, he took one quick glance my way and said, "Don't worry, nigga, I ain't no junkie." A booming baritone laugh escaped from deep down his chest, as if it was the sound of an enslaved soul finally set free, a total and complete contradiction of what Pyro's physical being represented. He cleared his throat and continued talking, gesturing toward the bank of closed-circuit TVs. "I know what you're thinking. How the fuck did this nigga install cameras on that highly guarded compound without anyone in the Zepeda crew catching wind of it? The answer to that question is simple. I had a nigga working for me on the inside who you may know as Ace. That's right, your homey was a double agent, helping me get intel on Tony's entire organization. All I had to do was arm him with a flash drive that he plugged into the facility's security camera's main computer terminal and *badda-bing, badda-boom*, I was in that ass like a thong, nigga." A huge smile cracked on Pyro's face as he marveled over his own genius. "Not only that, nigga, I could blow that entire facility to hell by just typing in a code on this console."

His words were making my head spin. I couldn't believe that an enemy of the Zepeda family would have that much control over the fate of their organization. It was mind boggling.

"Hold up, if you have the ability to destroy that facility, why haven't you done it yet?" I ask, watching Pyro's grin spread wider, exposing his gums.

"I was waiting for a purpose that was greater than my own. You see, as a soldier, one goes into battle not for oneself but for others. And today I have finally found a greater purpose other than myself." He stopped talking as he tapped on the console's keyboard. Suddenly the image of the facility's factory was replaced by an image of Sheila in an empty room, lying on her side on a concrete floor with her nightie on. My soul began to struggle within the confines of my body, trying to grab her through the monitor only to fail and become a tear sliding down my face.

"Easy there, beautiful demon. We'll get her back," said Pyro, with determination blazing in his eyes.

Part Two

Pyro

CHAPTER FOURTEEN

I couldn't help whistle John Philip Sousa's "Stars and Stripes Forever" as I disposed of Sammy's white van and the two Latino niggas that were following it.

"Ha, fucking amateurs," I scoffed, glancing at my rearview mirror at the two corpses whose necks bore the grotesque smile of death that only I could bring. From what I observed through that mirror, I slit their throats so bad that their tendons looked as if they were having a bit of difficulty trying to keep their heads attached to their necks. Their heads were tilted at grotesque angles that resembled that of an old jack-in-a-box spring that was worn out from age and dangled limply out of the left side of its box, as if waiting for someone put it back in.

"Top of the morning to ya, motherfuckers," I said in a mocking tone as I looked at the corpses through the rearview mirror. "It looks like y'all two need a bath in the Brandywine River," I quipped.

My mind quickly turned itself on autopilot. Starting up the engine, I let my mind roam free back to the memory of my two most recent kills (shit, Lord knows that I have done my fair share of "disposing" to know what route led to the Brandywine River, so I was straight).

Letting my mind rewind itself like an old VHS tape in a VCR, I went back to two hours prior, where I had left Sammy in a pitiful heap of despair in front of a huge screen displaying the love of his life lying unconscious in her nightie on the concrete floor of a cell. Shit, I was not going to front, watching Sammy touch that screen as if his hand had the power to transcend it and touch his beloved's cheek tugged at my heartstrings (what's left of them anyway). Shit, truth was, Sammy reminded me of Emanuel. He was my first and only true love, which was why I felt an overwhelming sense to protect and help Sammy get his girl back, if it was the last thing I did. On the real, it was because I feel this overwhelming sense in helping Sammy on his mission that I could sense Zepeda's goons a mile away. Taking my eyes away from the pitiful heap of Sammy lying on the floor in front of the monitor, I made my way toward the exit of my apartment, which was the basement of an old liquor store converted into a living space that was littered with photos of all my enemies and maps of their homes, place of businesses, and much more.

"How you holding up, Goldman?" I asked the man who slouched on the pea-green recliner in the middle of the room without taking my attention away from the rectangular gap that I used as a peephole to the steel door to see what was on the other side. So far, all that I could see was the darkness of night, open like the mouth of an endless chasm, but the soldier's instinct that was encompassing my body at the moment was gearing me up for a battle.

"Dawg, I'm just trying to hang in there," said Goldman, fatigue outlining his voice.

I turned away from the door to get a better look at him, hoping against hope that that glance that I would give him would somehow rejuvenate the man that sat in a pale broken-down heap of stab wounds and a bloodied undershirt, a shell of his former self. No longer did Goldman represent the self-assured young lawyer that he had once been. His eyes no longer shone with the intensity and pride of a man that seemed to have the law in his pocket. No, that was drained out of him when Tony Zepeda's men tortured him in that New Jersey motel room. In other words, the dude that I was looking at now was nothing less than a zombie version of himself, a dead man walking. The paleness that shrouded his being was an indicator that Goldman wasn't long for this world.

"How's our boy holding up?" said Goldman, nodding his head toward my war room, where Sammy Ortega kneeled in front a bank of CRT monitors that displayed the image of his love lying unconscious on a cold concrete floor. Pity surged through my body as I looked at the dude. With his gaze transfixed on the monitors, it was clear to me that at that very moment, Sammy's soul had left his body and was trying to transcend space and time to be with his beloved.

"Man, that's pitiful," said Goldman, shaking his head. "To think that emotional wreck back there was once considered one of the most feared hit men on the face of the earth," he said with a snort of disgust as his mind traveled to a much stronger and powerful image of Sammy.

"Yeah, well, pussy will do that to a man sometimes," I said with a sigh, turning my attention back to the front door; my soul was becoming anxious and preparing. *Any second now.* As if on cue, a beam of headlights glared past the peephole, catching my attention.

You stupid fucks, when you go to kill someone, you make sure that you cut off the damn headlights before you arrive on the scene. This thought bounced around the chambers of my mind, causing its loud echo to awaken my darkness.

"It's showtime, baby," I whispered to myself. The darkness inside began to climb from the pit of my stomach to the center of my heart, as if it was an anxious child that was in a rush to get home from school to play their new videogame console. Once the darkness settled comfortably deep within the cackles of my heart, I transformed into death itself, ready to destroy anything in my path.

Without giving it a second thought, I opened the door and quickly took cover against the cement wall that was a part of the staircase that led down to my basement apartment. Feeling the cool wall against my back, I let myself become reacquainted with the shadows that had protected me my entire life, my eternal armor.

"You sure this is where that nigga's hiding?" The question, drenched in a Spanish accent, floated to my ears from the black Honda Accord parked in the graveled parking lot. The windows from the driver's side door lowered completely, easily revealing the dude that I would soon kill.

"Weren't you paying attention, motherfucker? We've got surveillance on this faggot for days!"

"Jesus Christ, man. You need to calm the hell down. I was just asking a question."

From the sound of their bickering, it was easy to see that the two men did not have their attention on their mission, giving me ample time to sneak in the back seat of their car. Utilizing the sound of their bickering to shroud my movements on the parking lot gravel, I crouched and made my way toward one of the back doors of the Accord. Luckily, the door that I chose to enter from had its window partially down, allowing me to stick my hand down the opening and pop the lock up with my thumb and forefinger, thanking my lucky stars the car didn't have power locks. Quietly opening the door and making my way into the back seat, I swiftly removed the knife that I had concealed up my sleeve and with rapid movements, slit the throats of both men before they knew what hit them.

"Such fucking amateurs," I said, releasing a little snort of disgust at how incompetent those two were. Before I made my way out the car, I sat back in the middle of the seat to admire my handiwork. The blood spatter on the windshield was rather elegant to me, as the knife had penetrated the fleshy part of their necks, cutting both men in one swift and precise motion. Now, as I sat relaxed in the backseat, I observed how the two thick splatters of blood converged to form a crude rainbow-like arc on the windshield.

Oh, how gorgeous is that, I thought to myself. *The two blood splatters have merged into one.*

Overcome by an emotion that surged throughout my body, I couldn't help but notice the beauty on that windshield The two splatters of blood connecting as one. *A marriage in death*, I thought, letting the tears fall freely from my eyes.

"Damn, I gotta stop being so fucking sensitive," I said aloud, as my heart gripped to the last bit of that memory while the present was rapidly approaching. That final piece of memory was of me leaning forward in the backseat to touch the blood on the windshield. As the fingertips of my right hand touched the blood, I swear I could feel both of those men's souls swimming around in it, almost making all the joy and pain that they once held in the world palpable. In essence, I would say that by simply touching that blood smear, they became a part of me. I now owned them. Their souls were food for the grotesque monster that was my soul.

Yes, art at its finest. That was my final thought as I threw the two corpses in the river. "Bye, bye, my lovelies, you have served your purpose in my mission," I said in a dainty high-pitched voice, giving an effeminate wave to the corpses as they lazily rolled down the river.

CHAPTER FIFTEEN

The day had begun to open its eyes as I drove to a junkyard to dispose of Sammy's white van. Feeling the warm summer ray of the new day bathe my being, my thoughts turned back to Emanuel. A pang of longing overcame my heart and mind, bringing with it an overflow of memories that swept me away in its current. I once again turned my body on autopilot and let the current take me where it willed.

Suddenly I saw the face of my beloved. His lips full and plump always upturned in a slight smile, as if he was always enjoying a private joke the he came up with himself and refused to tell another living soul. His eyes would dance every time he would tell a story or say something philosophical that would catch the heart and make you melt. Emanuel was unlike any other individual that I had ever met in my life. The kid was a complete oxymoron, in my opinion. Although highly intelligent, he was confined to a wheelchair. That isn't to say that people confined to wheelchairs aren't intelligent, but Emanuel would often say this his mind felt prisoner to his body, blinding people to who he was. Noticing that I wasn't understanding what he was saying, he cleared throat and said, "When you first met me in our project lobby, what did you think of me?"

The answer to his question came quickly to my mind; however, I held myself back because I knew that my response might sting.

"I'll tell what you had thought of me that day," he said knowingly. "You more than likely felt sorry for me. Shit, maybe you were a little afraid to come near me for fear that my disability was contagious. Or perhaps you thought that retarded," he stated, hitting the nail on the head.

"Nah, I wasn't thinking that at all," I lied. "When I first saw you, I was thinking about how fly your electric wheelchair looked. On the real, I was kind of envious of your getting to drive in a life-size Tyco RC," I said jokingly.

"You lying asshole," Emanuel said, stifling a giggle. "You know damn well that you thought I was retarded. It's okay to admit that you felt that way, dude. Everyone thinks that about disabled people at least one time in their lives—that is, until they get to know us on a more personal level."

In all honesty, Emanuel was right. I did indeed stereotype him when I first saw him racing out of our lobby chasing after a female crackhead that was so skinny she resembled a corpse whose body had long picked clean by the maggots in its grave, except that corpse had been reanimated and was running full speed toward the exit with Emanuel's neon red backpack in hand.

"Come back here with my shit, bitch," he'd screamed, his voice thick with rage, bouncing off the acoustics of the lobby.

Witnessing this, I ran toward the woman, tackling her inches away from the exit.

"Get off of me, motherfucker," screamed the woman. Her cries were guttural and shrill, like a wounded animal that got its paw caught in a bear trap. Turning her on her back, I swung my right fist and connected with her jaw, causing a grotesque shatter to be the new sound to bounce off the lobby's acoustics. Snatching the backpack from her limp hand, I turned my gaze toward the wheezing sound of the electric wheelchair coming straight at me, inches from my face.

"Hey, thanks, man," he said this to me, snatching his backpack in a brisk motion while trying to wipe the drool dripping down his chin. Honest to God, Emanuel scared the hell out of me at that moment. I thought he had contracted rabies. Failing to hide my fear from him, I quickly snatched my hand back for fear that he might bite it.

Noticing my fear, Emanuel said, "Dude, you don't have to be afraid me. I promise that I won't bite you. If it's the drool that frightens you, I can assure that nothing is wrong with me. Unfortunately, this ghastly drooling is a side effect of my cerebral palsy. I know that I look crazy and retarded, but I can't help it," he said, lowering his eyes in shame.

It was then that Emanuel's gaze landed on the grotesque burn scars that riddled my arm, causing it to resemble that of a geriatric man.

"What happened to your arm, dude?" Emanuel's question began to open a scar of a memory, causing it to bleed out visions of my father making me put my entire right arm on the stove. It wasn't enough for him to just put my hand. Shaking my head as if to dislodge the memory from my mind, I turned my attention back to the crackhead that was pinned under me. The woman's jaw was visibly broken, its lower half resembling that of an old wooden dummy that laid abandoned in its owner's magic trunk for years.

"Let me go, motherfucker," the crackhead woman said weakly through her slack jaw. Pity for her started to fill my heart. Letting my emotions get the best of me, I lessened my weight on her, letting the woman slip out from me as I stood up. Without a word, she quickly got to her feet and ran out of the blobby as if demons were chasing her out of hell. A smile creased my features as I watch the woman run north toward Market Street.

Turning to face Emanuel, I finally caught a full glimpse of his features, His hair was slicked back with gel, reminding me of a 1950s greaser. His eyes seemed to sparkle with a vibrant light that seemed to radiate throughout his entire being. It was like his soul was coming out to greet me, letting me partake in its beauty. His mouth was outlined with beautiful plump lips the color of salmon, just begging to be kissed. I couldn't take it much longer. I needed to touch him *so that I could obtain some of his beauty,* but I didn't want to come off weird or offensive. To my surprise, however, Emanuel grabbed my scarred arm and kissed it, leaving his lips pressed upon it for a full twenty seconds with his eyes closed.

When releasing my arm, he opened his eyes and said, "I can feel your pain. Please share it with me. If you ever want to talk or anything, I'm in apartment 1-A. I'm always home if you need me."

With that, he backed up his wheelchair and speeded out the exit into the morning sun, leaving me with tears running down my face. It was right then and there that I fell in love with Emanuel and wanted desperately to bask in the aura of his beauty. It was as if my soul was climbing out of my eyes and down my cheeks to grab some of his beauty and abscond with it.

Following the week after the incident in our project lobby, I took Emanuel up on his offer and visited his apartment. It was as though my soul was attracted to the light that radiated behind that door. I was a moth to a flame. To put it mildly, my visits to Emanuel's were nourishment to my soul, allowing my emaciated soul to gorge on the feast that was his love and intelligence. For it was during such visits that he would school me on the great philosopher, while eating rice and beans or *arroz con pollo* (I loved Puerto Rican food). Emanuel once explained to me that a psychologist named Viktor Frankl stated that to live was to suffer and to survive meant that we must discover the meaning in our suffering. Touched by the profound meaning of those, tears of shame fell freely from my eyes as I confessed to him that Otis, my stepfather, would come into my room at night and rape me, forcing his old smelly dick to rip through my asshole, making it bleed the first time he attacked me. Not only did he repeatedly rape me, but he would also lock me up in a kennel cage whenever I disobeyed him, forcing me to eat my excrement.

With tears stinging my eyes, I also confessed to Emanuel that I had slit my stepfather's throat as he slept on the living room couch. Disposing of Otis's body was a breeze. Due to my Uncle George's job at Delaware Waste Management as a garbage collector (he also hated Otis with passion for beating my mom to death and throwing her down a flight of stairs), he helped me wrap the body in a huge garbage bag, throwing it in a dumpster so that the garbage truck he worked on could pick it up the next morning.

"Man, that's some serious shit," said Emanuel, his eyes as big as saucers. I could feel the mixture of horror and amazement conjure grotesque murder scenes in his mind, making me smile.

"Don't sweat it, nigga, I ain't no crazed maniac. I just had to do what I had to do," I said in a casual tone, as if I just told him that I had returned from the grocery store a few minutes ago.

"Just so you know, your secret is safe with me," said Emanuel in a low paternal tone, letting his words wash over me like warm soapy water. I can honestly admit that at that very moment, I felt the safest I had ever been in my entire life, so safe, in fact, that I let myself be driven by impulse and emotion and kissed Emanuel passionately. It was on that day that we declared our love for one another.

CHAPTER SIXTEEN

The memory of our first kiss began to dissolve into the present day. No longer was I in Emanuel's apartment sharing a kiss, but out on the open road driving a van to a junkyard to be destroyed. I could feel my heart start to capsize with the weight of the emotion it carried in a sea of anger that was now forming a tidal wave that consumed me with rage.

"Goddamn you, Sammy! You were the one who took my love away from me. You were the motherfucker who murdered Emanuel in cold blood." I said all this out loud as images of Sammy shooting Emanuel in the chest flashed before my mind's eyes, causing me to pull the van over to the side of the road before I lost control. Punching the steering wheel with all my might, I managed to break the van's horn. This caused it to sound an everlasting honk, as if someone were resting their hand on it for an eternity, making it sound like an eternal wail of pain.

With tears streaming down my eyes, I noticed that the van had run out of gas. I hopped out of the van and stood in the middle of the road as a red sedan Ford coming up the road. Noticing this, I quickly pulled my 9mm pistol from my waistband and waited as the car came to a screeching in front of me. I pointed my pistol directly at the young woman driving the car. Frozen in fear, the young woman didn't get out the car until I went over to the driver's side door, snatching her by her silky blonde hair and pulling her entire petite frame out of the driver side window. Before she could let out a scream for help, I snapped her neck, throwing her lifeless body to the asphalt and noticing how stunning she looked in her black leggings and dark green crop top.

"Such a cute little white chick," I said sympathetically to myself as I opened the door and got behind the wheel, thankful that the road was practically deserted. Abandoning my original plan of destroying the van, I turned the car around and headed back home, ready to finish this once and for all.

CHAPTER SEVENTEEN

"Wwhat's good, man?" said the male voice on the other end of the phone line after five rings.

"Nigga, what took you so long to pick up your damn phone, I said angrily, letting my street language slip out.

"Shit, you sound just like my main ho when I don't answer her calls right away."

"Look, motherfucker, this is some serious shit I have planned out, and it's all coming together. I don't need shitheads like you fucking it up," I said, scolding my henchman like an unruly child.

"Yo, you better shut down all that noise, dude," the man on the other end of the phone said, with anger rising in his voice. "Just so your ass knows, I had to subdue your little friend. He tried to leave the apartment, so I shot him."

"You did what!" I yelled, swerving the red sedan into the opposite lane, almost crashing head-on with a Greyhound bus. "Nigga, tell me you didn't kill the bastard, please? My voice was now drenched in a pleading shrill.

"Pyro, you need to relax, man. I just blew out both of his knee-caps with my trusty double-barrel shotgun." The man on the other side of the phone said this, letting the final words of that sentence be engulfed in bubbles of laughter. "I didn't kill the dude, all right. As soon as I saw him fall on his back, I picked him up and tied him up in the basement where the girl's at, just like you told me to. There's a problem, though. Your boy Goldman is dead. Yeah, the nigga must have bled out or something. I found him torn the fuck up in that ugly ass-green chair you got in your living room."

"Oh well, the man served his purpose," I said nonchalantly. Goldman was just a pawn in my game. I had no further use for him whatsoever. The same could be said for the man on the other end of the phone who had followed me around since the war with Iraq. His name was Jamal Mahammad, an African American Muslim on my platoon who was disgruntled with how Muslims were treated in America. The poor bastard let himself be brainwashed by me, believing I was going to start some sort of militia in the name of Allah. Little did he know, however, that once I ended the call abruptly without his knowledge, his cell phone would explode, dislodging shrapnel in his brain. A rather ingenious explosive that I invented, I thought to myself, hanging up my cell without saying goodbye.

My mind raced with images of Jamal holding his ear as his eyes rolled back into his head while foaming at the mouth due to brain damage. It was kind of sad to think that the only body the authorities would find intact after this would be Jamal's due to the fact that he was in an old apartment that was on the premises of the abandoned liquor store that I lived under.

CHAPTER EIGHTEEN

Arriving at my place, I could hardly contain my excitement. My palms were sweaty. I could feel my heart bang wildly against my rib cage, causing me to lose focus and talk to myself. "Oh my god, oh my god! You will be avenged today, Emanuel. I will be by your side soon, baby!" This all came out of me in a singsong voice as I made my way into my apartment.

Opening the front door, I was greeted by the grotesque image of Goldman's corpse lying slumped over in the easy chair as if he were sleeping. The wounds of his injuries open and gaping like the mouths of screaming banshees. The bloodstains on his shirt, once a shade of crimson, were now brown with a day of age. Forgetting about the horrific tableau that was before me, I made my way to the small kitchen in the back of my apartment where there was a man-hole-like cover hiding a tunnel that I had been digging for about a year now, day and night, hoping that it wouldn't cave in on me.

Making my way down the rope ladder, I could feel Emanuel's presence all around me, comforting and giving me power beyond belief. Reaching the end of the rope ladder, my feet touched linoleum floor along with white brick walls. The whiteness on them was so bright that it hurt my eyes. Truth be told, if I hadn't built that dungeon myself, I would have sworn that I was on the set of the first *Saw* movie. Chained up to the wall in front of me were an unconscious Sammy and Sheila, both of their heads dangling on their necks as if overtaken by sleep. Before walking any closer to my victims, I took the time to observe Jamal's handiwork. Both the arms and legs of my victims were tied firmly, reminding me of Christ on the cross.

"Perfect," I muttered, stepping closer to Sammy, smacking him awake. Seeing the dazed and confused look on his face brought so much joy to me, I couldn't help but let out a little giggle.

"Wake up, beautiful demon," I said, watching Sammy shake the grogginess away.

His eyes took in the room and asked, "What the fuck," Pyro?" He asked the question in such a calm tone that I had to laugh.

"Do you know why you are here?" I asked with a broad smile, but in place of an answer, I got a scream as he noticed Sheila right beside him.

"Oh, God, please don't hurt her," Sammy pleaded as his eyes landed on his beloved.

"It's funny that you should say that. I felt the same exact way when you killed Emanuel. Did you have mercy on him? It wasn't his fault that his dad owed drug money to Zepeda, but you killed him anyway as a message to his father. Well, guess what? Emanuel's father didn't give a rat's ass about his son. That just give him more time to hide. Did you ever catch the bastard, by the way? No, you did not, but I did. He was holed up in a whorehouse in old San Juan. Yeah, I sliced his throat from ear to ear and stabbed to death the chick he was fucking. I know what you're asking yourself right now—what was so important about a crippled teenager, right? Well, he was my lover. He taught me how to be human. He taught me I have self-worth. Hell, Emanuel even taught me how to speak proper English. The kid would often tell me that the worst part of living in the ghetto was that ignorance is often championed over intelligence. I swear, it was like Emanuel had a force field that would protect him from the ghetto—that is, until you killed him. I was there hiding behind the couch like a coward. It took me twenty-two years to set this moment up, but I did it. I was the one that pulled the strings to get you out of jail. I used Goldman to buy off the judge on your case to set you free. By the way, while you were in the joint, I wiped out Zepeda's entire crew, establishing me the head of the Delaware's drug trade."

I stopped talking, catching my breath as I dug my phone out of my back pocket. "To show you it is not all ill will toward you, I will read an excerpt from a review from your book." I cleared my throat and began to read from my phone.

"'Not since *Fifty Shades of Grey* has a book made such an impact on its readers. Never before has a street biography touched the heart of so many with its poetic prose...'" It was at that moment that I could feel the anger boil up in my chest, and I stopped reading, taking out my pistol and shooting both Sammy and Sheila in the chest.

Giggling like a madman, I got down on my knees and yelled, "Emanuel, you are avenged, my love." Putting the pistol to my temple, I pulled the trigger and let darkness consume me.

CPSIA information can be obtained
at www.ICGtesting.com
Printed in the USA
BVHW070922070421
604343BV00005B/897

Mediterranean
Recipe Collection

Quick and Easy Recipes
To Weight Loss

Ben Cooper

Table of Contents

Hummus with Ground Lamb

Preparation Time: 10 minutes
Cooking Time: 15 minute
Servings: 8

Ingredients:

10 oz. hummus
12 oz. lamb meat, ground
½ cup pomegranate seeds
¼ cup parsley, chopped
1 tbsp. olive oil
Pita chips for serving

Directions:

1.Heat a pan with the oil over medium-high heat, add the meat, and brown for 15 minutes stirring often.

2.Spread the hummus on a platter, spread the ground lamb all over, and spread the pomegranate seeds and the parsley and serve with pita chips.

Wrapped Plums Preparation

Preparation Time: 5 minutes
Cooking Time: 0 minutes
Servings: 8

Ingredients:

2 oz. prosciutto, cut into 16 pieces
4 plums, quartered
1 tbsp. chives, chopped
A pinch of red pepper flakes, crushed

Directions:

1.Wrap each plum quarter in a prosciutto slice, arrange them all on a platter, sprinkle the chives and pepper flakes all over and serve.

Cucumber Sandwich Bites

Preparation Time: 5 minutes
Cooking Time: 0 minutes
Servings: 12

Ingredients:

1 cucumber, sliced
8 slices whole wheat bread
2 tbsp. cream cheese, soft
1 tbsp. chives, chopped
¼ cup avocado, peeled, pitted and mashed
1 tsp. mustard
Salt and black pepper to the taste

Directions:

1.Spread the mashed avocado on each bread slice, also spread the rest of the ingredients except the cucumber slices.

2.Divide the cucumber slices on the bread slices, cut each slice in thirds, arrange on a platter and serve as an appetizer.

Cucumber Rolls

Preparation Time: 5 minutes
Cooking Time: 0 minutes
Servings: 6

Ingredients:

1 big cucumber, sliced lengthwise
1 tbsp. parsley, chopped
8 oz. canned tuna, drained and mashed
Salt and black pepper to the taste
1 tsp. lime juice

Directions:

1.Arrange cucumber slices on a working surface, divide the rest of the ingredients, and roll.

2.Arrange all the rolls on a platter and serve as an appetizer.

Olives and Cheese Stuffed Tomatoes

Preparation Time: 10 minutes
Cooking Time: 0 minutes
Servings: 24

Ingredients:

24 cherry tomatoes, top cut off and insides scooped out
2 tbsp. olive oil
¼ tsp. red pepper flakes
½ cup feta cheese, crumbled
2 tbsp. black olive paste
¼ cup mint, torn

Directions:

1.In a bowl, mix the olives paste with the rest of the ingredients except the cherry tomatoes and whisk. Stuff the cherry tomatoes with this mix, arrange them all on a platter and serve as an appetizer.

Tomato Salsa

Preparation Time: 5 minutes
Cooking Time: 0 minutes
Servings: 6

Ingredients:

1 garlic clove, minced
4 tbsp. olive oil
5 tomatoes, cubed
1 tbsp. balsamic vinegar
¼ cup basil, chopped
1 tbsp. parsley, chopped
1 tbsp. chives, chopped
Salt and black pepper to the taste
Pita chips for serving

Directions:

1.In a bowl, mix the tomatoes with the garlic and the rest of the ingredients except the pita chips, stir, divide into small cups and serve with the pita chips on the side.

Chili Mango and Watermelon Salsa

Preparation Time: 5 minutes
Cooking Time: 0 minutes
Servings: 12

Ingredients:

1 red tomato, chopped
Salt and black pepper to the taste
1 cup watermelon, seedless, peeled and cubed
1 red onion, chopped
2 mangos, peeled and chopped
2 chili peppers, chopped
¼ cup cilantro, chopped
3 tbsp. lime juice
Pita chips for serving

Directions:

1.In a bowl, mix the tomato with the watermelon, the onion and the rest of the ingredients except the pita chips and toss well.

2.Divide the mix into small cups and serve with pita chips on the side.

Creamy Spinach and Shallots Dip

Preparation Time: 10 minutes
Cooking Time: 0 minutes
Servings: 4

Ingredients:

1 lb. spinach, roughly chopped
2 shallots, chopped
2 tbsp. mint, chopped
¾ cup cream cheese, soft
Salt and black pepper to the taste

Directions:

1.In a blender, combine the spinach with the shallots and the rest of the ingredients, and pulse well.

2. Divide into small bowls and serve as a party dip.

Feta Artichoke

Preparation Time: 10 minutes

Cooking Time: 30 minutes

Servings: 8

Ingredients:

8 oz. artichoke hearts, drained and quartered
¾ cup basil, chopped
¾ cup green olives, pitted and chopped
1 cup parmesan cheese, grated
5 oz. feta cheese, crumbled

Directions:

1.In your food processor, mix the artichokes with the basil and the rest of the ingredients, pulse well, and transfer to a baking dish.

2.Introduce in the oven, bake at 375° F for 30 minutes and serve as a party dip.

Chickpeas and Beets Mix

Preparation Time: 10 minutes
Cooking Time: 25 minutes
Servings: 4

Ingredients:

3 tablespoons capers, drained and chopped Juice of 1 lemon
Zest of 1 lemon, grated
1 red onion, chopped
3 tablespoons olive oil
14 ounces canned chickpeas, drained 8 ounces beets, peeled and cubed
1 tablespoon parsley, chopped
Salt and pepper to the taste

Directions:

1.Heat a pan with the oil over medium heat, add the onion, lemon zest, lemon juice and the capers and sauté for 5 minutes.

2.Add the rest of the ingredients, stir and cook over medium-low heat for 20 minutes more.

3.Divide the mix between plates and serve as a side dish.

Creamy Sweet Potatoes Mix

Preparation Time: 10 minutes
Cooking Time: 1 hour
Servings: 4

Ingredients:

4 tablespoons olive oil
1 garlic clove, minced
4 medium sweet potatoes, pricked with a fork
1 red onion, sliced
3 ounces baby spinach
Zest and juice of 1 lemon
A small bunch dill, chopped
1 and ½ tablespoons Greek yogurt
2 tablespoons tahini paste
Salt and black pepper to the taste

Directions:

1.Put the potatoes on a baking sheet lined with parchment paper, introduce in the oven at 350 degrees F and cook them for 1 hour.

2.Peel the potatoes, cut them into wedges and put them in a bowl.

3.Add the garlic, the oil and the rest of the ingredients, toss, divide the mix between plates and serve.

Cabbage and Mushrooms Mix

Preparation Time: 10 minutes
Cooking Time: 15 minutes
Servings: 2

Ingredients:

1 yellow onion, sliced
2 tablespoons olive oil
1 tablespoon balsamic vinegar
½ pound white mushrooms, sliced
1 green cabbage head, shredded
4 spring onions, chopped
Salt and black pepper to the taste

Directions:

1. Heat a pan with the oil over medium heat, add the yellow onion and the spring onions and cook for 5 minutes.

2. Add the rest of the ingredients, cook everything for 10 minutes, divide between plates and serve.

Lemon Mushroom Rice

Preparation Time: 10 minutes
Cooking Time: 30 minutes
Servings: 4

Ingredients:

2 cups chicken stock
1 yellow onion, chopped
½ pound white mushrooms, sliced
2 garlic cloves, minced
8 ounces wild rice
Juice and zest of 1 lemon
1 tablespoon chives, chopped
6 tablespoons goat cheese, crumbled
Salt and black pepper to the taste

Directions:

1.Heat a pot with the stock over medium heat, add the rice, onion and the rest of the ingredients except the chives and the cheese, bring to a simmer and cook for 25 minutes.

2.Add the remaining ingredients, cook everything for 5 minutes, divide between plates and serve as a side dish.

Paprika and Chives Potatoes

Preparation Time: 10 minutes
Cooking Time: 1 hour and 8 minutes
Servings: 4

Ingredients:

4 potatoes, scrubbed and pricked with a fork
1 tablespoon olive oil
1 celery stalk, chopped 2 tomatoes, chopped
1 teaspoon sweet paprika
Salt and black pepper to the taste
2 tablespoons chives, chopped

Directions:

1.Arrange the potatoes on a baking sheet lined with parchment paper, introduce in the oven and bake at 350 degrees F for 1 hour.

2.Cool the potatoes down, peel and cut them into larger cubes.

3.Heat a pan with the oil over medium heat, add the celery and the tomatoes and sauté for 2 minutes.

4.Add the potatoes and the rest of the ingredients, toss, cook everything for 6 minutes, divide the mix between plates and serve as a side dish.

Bulgur, Kale and Cheese Mix
Preparation Time: 10 minutes
Cooking Time: 10 minutes
Servings: 6

Ingredients:

4 ounces bulgur
4 ounces kale, chopped
1 tablespoon mint, chopped
3 spring onions, chopped
1 cucumber, chopped
A pinch of allspice, ground
2 tablespoons olive oil
Zest and juice of ½ lemon
4 ounces feta cheese, crumbled

Directions:

1.Put bulgur in a bowl, cover with hot water, aside for 10 minutes and fluff with a fork.

2.Heat a pan with the oil over medium heat, add the onions and the allspice and cook for 3 minutes.

3.Add the bulgur and the rest of the ingredients, cook everything for 5-6 minutes more, divide between plates and serve.

Spicy Green Beans Mix

Preparation Time: 5 minutes
Cooking Time: 15 minutes
Servings: 4

Ingredients:

4 teaspoons olive oil
1 garlic clove, minced
½ teaspoon hot paprika
¾ cup veggie stock
1 yellow onion, sliced
1 pound green beans, trimmed and halved
½ cup goat cheese, shredded
2 teaspoon balsamic vinegar

Directions:

1.Heat a pan with the oil over medium heat, add the garlic, stir and cook for 1 minute.

2.Add the green beans and the rest of the ingredients, toss, cook everything for 15 minutes more, divide between plates and serve as a side dish.

Beans and Rice

Preparation Time: 10 minutes
Cooking Time: 55 minutes
Servings: 6

Ingredients:

1 tablespoon olive oil
1 yellow onion, chopped
2 celery stalks, chopped
2 garlic cloves, minced
2 cups brown rice
1 and ½ cup canned black beans, rinsed and drained
4 cups water
Salt and black pepper to the taste

Directions:

1.Heat a pan with the oil over medium heat, add the celery, garlic and the onion, stir and cook for 10 minutes.

2.Add the rest of the ingredients, stir, bring to a simmer and cook over medium heat for 45 minutes.

3.Divide between plates and serve.

Tomato and Millet Mix

Preparation Time: 10 minutes
Cooking Time: 20 minutes
Servings: 6

Ingredients:

3 tablespoons olive oil
1 cup millet
2 spring onions, chopped
2 tomatoes, chopped
½ cup cilantro, chopped
1 teaspoon chili paste
6 cups cold water
½ cup lemon juice
Salt and black pepper to the taste

Directions:

1.Heat a pan with the oil over medium heat, add the millet, stir and cook for 4 minutes.

2.Add the water, salt and pepper, stir, and bring a simmer over medium heat cook for 15 minutes.

3.Add the rest of the ingredients, toss, divide the mix between plates and serve as a side dish.

Quinoa and Greens Salad

Preparation Time: 10 minutes
Cooking Time: 0 minutes
Servings: 4

Ingredients:

1 cup quinoa, cooked
1 medium bunch collard greens, chopped
4 tablespoons walnuts, chopped
2 tablespoons balsamic vinegar
4 tablespoons tahini paste
4 tablespoons cold water
A pinch of salt and black pepper
1 tablespoon olive oil

Directions:

1.In a bowl, mix the tahini with the water and vinegar
and whisk.

2.In a bowl, mix the quinoa with the rest of the
ingredients and the tahini dressing, toss, divide the mix
between plates and serve as a side dish.

Veggies and Avocado Dressing

Preparation Time: 10 minutes
Cooking Time: 0 minutes
Servings: 4

Ingredients:

3 tablespoons pepitas, roasted
3 cups water
2 tablespoons cilantro, chopped
4 tablespoons parsley, chopped
1 and ½ cups corn
1 cup radish, sliced
2 avocados, peeled, pitted and chopped
2 mangos, peeled and chopped
3 tablespoons olive oil
4 tablespoons Greek yogurt
1 teaspoons balsamic vinegar
2 tablespoons lime juice
Salt and black pepper to the taste

Directions:

1.In your blender, mix the olive oil with avocados, salt, pepper, lime juice, the yogurt and the vinegar and pulse.

2.In a bowl, mix the pepitas with the cilantro, parsley and the rest of the ingredients, and toss.

3.Add the avocado dressing, toss, divide the mix between plates and serve as a side dish.

Guacamole

Preparation Time: 10 minutes
Cooking Time: 0 minutes
Servings: 4

Ingredients:

3 avocados - peeled, seeded and mashed
1 lime, juiced
1 teaspoon salt
1/2 cup diced onion
3 tablespoons chopped fresh coriander
2 Roma tomatoes, diced
1 teaspoon chopped garlic
1 pinch of ground cayenne pepper (optional)

Directions:

1.Puree avocados, lime juice, and salt in a medium bowl.

2.Stir in the onion, coriander, tomatoes, and garlic. Stir in the cayenne pepper.

Sugar-coated Pecans

Preparation Time: 15 minutes
Cooking Time: 1 hour
Servings: 12

Ingredients:

1 egg white
1 tablespoon water
1 pound pecan halves
1 cup white sugar
3/4 teaspoon salt
1/2 teaspoon ground cinnamon

Directions:

1.Preheat the oven to 120 ° C (250 ° F). Grease a baking tray.

2.In a bowl, whisk the egg whites and water until frothy. Combine the sugar, salt, and cinnamon in another bowl.

3.Add the pecans to the egg whites and stir to cover the nuts.

4.Remove the nuts and mix them with the sugar until well covered. Spread the nuts on the prepared baking sheet.

5.Bake for 1 hour at 250 ° F (120 ° C). Stir every 15 minutes.

Southwestern Egg Rolls

Preparation Time: 20 minutes
Cooking Time: 20 minutes
Servings: 5

Ingredients:

2 tablespoons vegetable oil
1/2 chicken fillet, skinless
2 tablespoons chopped green onion
2 tablespoons chopped red pepper
1/3 cup frozen corn kernels
1/4 cup black beans, rinsed and drained
2 tablespoons chopped frozen spinach, thawed and drained
2 tablespoons diced jalapeño peppers
1/2 tablespoon chopped fresh parsley
1/2 c. ground cumin
1/2 teaspoon chili powder
1/3 teaspoon salt
1 pinch of ground cayenne pepper
3/4 cup of grated Monterey Jack cheese
5 flour tortillas (6 inches)
1 liter of oil for frying

Directions:

1.Rub 1 tablespoon of vegetable oil on the chicken fillet.

2.Cook the chicken in a medium-sized saucepan over medium heat for about 5 minutes per side until the meat is no longer pink and the juice is clear.

3.Remove from heat and set aside.

4.Heat 1 tablespoon of remaining vegetable oil in a medium-sized saucepan over medium heat. Stir in the green onion and red pepper. Boil and stir for 5 minutes, until soft.

5.Cut the diced chicken and mix in the pan with the onion and red pepper. Mix corn, black beans, spinach, jalapeño pepper, parsley, cumin, chili powder, salt, and cayenne pepper.

6.Boil and stir for 5 minutes, until everything is well mixed and soft. Remove from heat and stir in Monterey Jack cheese until it melts.

7..Wrap the tortillas with a clean, slightly damp cloth — microwave at maximum power, about 1 minute, or until it is hot and malleable.

8..Pour equal amounts of the mixture into each tortilla.

9..Fold the ends of the tortillas and wrap the mixture well. Safe with toothpicks. Arrange in a medium-sized dish, cover with plastic, and place in the freezer. Freeze for at least 4 hours.

10.Heat the oil in a deep frying pan to 190° C for frying. Bake frozen stuffed tortillas for 10 minutes or until golden brown. Drain on paper towels before serving.

Annie's Salsa Chips with Fruit & Cinnamon

Preparation Time: 15 minutes
Cooking Time: 15 minutes
Servings: 10

Ingredients:

2 Golden Delicious apples - peeled, seeded and diced
8 grams of raspberry
2 kiwis, peeled and diced
1 pound of strawberries
2 tablespoons of white sugar
1 tablespoon of brown sugar
3 tablespoons canned fruit Flour cooking aerosol
Flour tortillas
2 tablespoons cinnamon sugar

Directions:

1.Combine kiwi, Golden Delicious apples, raspberries, strawberries, white sugar, brown sugar, and canned fruit in a large bowl. Cover and put in the fridge for at least 15 minutes.

2.Preheat the oven to 175 ° C (350 ° F).
Cover one side of each flour tortilla with a cooking spray.

3.Cut into segments and place them in one layer on a large baking sheet. Sprinkle the quarters with the desired amount of cinnamon sugar. Spray again with cooking spray.

4.Bake in the preheated oven for 8 to 10 minutes.
Repeat this with the other tortilla quarters.

5.Cool for approximately 15 minutes. Serve with a
mixture of
fresh fruit.

Boneless Buffalo Wings

Preparation Time: 10 minutes
Cooking Time: 15 minutes
Servings: 3

Ingredients:

Frying oil
1 cup unbleached flour
2 teaspoons of salt
1/2 teaspoon ground black pepper
1/2 teaspoon cayenne pepper
1/4 teaspoon garlic powder
1/2 teaspoon bell pepper
1 egg
1 cup of milk
3 boneless chicken fillets, skinless, cut into 1/2 inch strips
1/4 cup hot pepper sauce
1 tablespoon butter

Directions:

1.Heat the oil in a frying pan or large saucepan.

2.Mix the flour, salt, black pepper, cayenne pepper, garlic powder, and bell pepper in a large bowl. Beat the egg and milk in a small bowl.

3Dip each piece of chicken in the egg mixture and then roll it into the flour mixture.

4.Repeat the process so that each piece of chicken is doubled. Cool the breaded chicken for 20 minutes.

5.Fry chicken in hot oil, in batches. Cook until the outside is well browned and the juice is clear, 5 to 6 minutes per batch.

6.Mix the hot sauce and butter in a small bowl. Heat the sauce in the microwave on high to melt, 20 to 30 seconds. Pour the sauce over the cooked chicken; mix well.

Jalapeño Popper Spread

Preparation Time: 10 minutes
Cooking Time: 3 minutes
Servings: 32

Ingredients:

2 packets of cream cheese, softened
1 cup mayonnaise
1 (4-gram) can chopped green peppers, drained
2 grams diced jalapeño peppers, canned, drained
1 cup grated Parmesan cheese

Directions:

1.In a large bowl, mix cream cheese and mayonnaise until smooth. Stir the bell peppers and jalapeño peppers.

2.Pour the mixture into a microwave oven and sprinkle with Parmesan cheese. Microwave on maximum power, about 3 minutes.

Brown Sugar Smokies

Preparation Time: 10 minutes
Cooking Time: 10 minutes
Servings: 12

Ingredients:

1 pound bacon
1 (16 ounces) package little smoky sausages
1 cup brown sugar, or to taste

Directions:

1.Preheat the oven to 175 ° C (350 ° F).

2.Cut the bacon in three and wrap each strip around a little sausage.

3.Place sausages wrapped on wooden skewers, several to one place the kebabs on a baking sheet and sprinkle generously with brown sugar.

4.Bake until the bacon is crispy, and the brown sugar has melted.

Pita Chips

Preparation Time: 10 minutes
Cooking Time: 8 minutes
Servings: 24

Ingredients:

12 slices of pita bread
1/2 cup of olive oil
1/2 teaspoon ground black pepper
1 teaspoon garlic salt
1/2 teaspoon dried basil
1 teaspoon dried chervil

Directions:

1.Preheat the oven to 200 degrees C (400 degrees F).

2.Cut each pita bread into 8 triangles. Place the triangles on the baking sheet.

3.Combine oil, pepper, salt, basil, and chervil in a small bowl. Brush each triangle with the oil mixture.

4.Bake in the preheated oven for about 7 minutes or until light brown and crispy.

Hot Spinach, Artichoke & Chili Dip

Preparation Time: 10 minutes
Cooking Time: 30 minutes
Servings: 10

Ingredients:

2 (8 oz.) packages of cream cheese, softened
1/2 cup of mayonnaise
1 can (4.5 oz.) chopped green pepper, drained
1 cup of freshly grated Parmesan cheese
1 jar (12 oz.) marinated artichoke hearts, drained and chopped
1/4 cup canned chopped jalapeño peppers, drained
1 can of chopped spinach frozen, thawed and drained

Directions:

1.Preheat the oven to 175 ° C (350 ° F).

2.Mix the cream cheese and mayonnaise in a bowl. Stir the green peppers, parmesan cheese, artichokes, peppers, and spinach.

3.Pour the mixture into a baking dish.

4.Bake in the preheated oven until light brown, about 30 minutes.

Fruit Dip

Preparation Time: 5 minutes
Cooking Time: 0 minutes
Servings: 12

Ingredients:

1 (8-oz.) package cream cheese, softened
1 (7-oz.) jar marshmallow crème

Directions:

1.Use an electric mixer to combine the cream cheese and marshmallow Beat until everything is well mixed.

Banana & Tortilla Snacks

Preparation Time: 5 minutes
Cooking Time: 0 minutes
Servings: 1

Ingredients:

1 flour tortilla (6 inches)
2 tablespoons peanut butter
1 tablespoon honey
1 banana
2 tablespoons raisins

Directions:

1.Lay the tortilla flat. Spread peanut butter and honey on the tortilla.

2.Place the banana in the middle and sprinkle the raisins.

3.Wrap and serve.

Wonton Snacks

Preparation Time: 20 minutes
Cooking Time: 12 minutes
Servings: 48

Ingredients:

2 pounds of ground pork
2 stalks of celery
2 carrots
2 cloves of garlic
1 small onion
1 (8-gram) can water chestnuts
1/2 cup of Thai peanut sauce prepared
1 package (14-oz.) wonton wraps

Directions:

1.Finely chop celery, carrots, garlic, onion and water chestnuts in a food processor. Parts must be small and fairly uniform, but not liquid.

2.Mix ground pork and chopped vegetables in a large frying pan.

3.Cook over medium heat until the vegetables are soft and the pork is no longer pink.

4.Turn up the heat and let the moisture evaporate, then add the peanut sauce and cook for another 5 minutes before removing it from the heat.

5.While cooking the pork mixture, preheat the oven to 175 ° C (350 ° F).

6.Press a wonton wrap into each cup of a mini muffin pan, with flared edges on the sides.

7.Place a spoonful of the meat mixture in each cup.

8.Bake in the preheated oven for about 12 minutes or until the outer envelopes are crispy and golden brown.

Sesame Stick Snacks

Preparation Time: 15 minutes
Cooking Time: 15 minutes
Servings: 10

Ingredients:

2 cups biscuit baking mix
2/3 cup heavy cream
1/4 cup butter, melted
1 1/2 tablespoons sesame seeds

Directions:

1.Preheat the oven to 220 ° C. Lightly grease 2 baking trays.

2.Mix the dough mixture and the cream; mix for 30 seconds.

3.Turn the dough on a lightly floured surface and knead 10 times. Roll the dough into a 5 x 10- inch rectangle.

4.Cut the dough into 1/2 inch wide strips.

5.Place the strips on prepared baking trays. Brush the strips with melted butter and sprinkle with sesame seeds.

6.Bake in the preheated oven for 15 minutes, until golden brown.

Shawn's Study Snacks

Preparation Time: 10 minutes
Cooking Time: 10 minutes
Servings: 60

Ingredients:

3 bananas, pureed
3/4 cup butter
1 egg
1 cup of white sugar
1/4 cup of packaged brown sugar
1 teaspoon baking powder
2 1/2 cups flour
1/4 teaspoon ground nutmeg
1/2 teaspoon ground cinnamon
1 1/2 cups oatmeal
3/4 cup chopped walnuts
1/2 cup raisins (optional)

Directions:

1.Preheat the oven to 175 ° C (350 ° F).
Mix in order, making sure the butter or margarine is well absorbed. More flour can be added if needed.

2.Spoon soup on a greased baking sheet. Bake for 10 minutes or until the edges are light brown.

Pistachio Arugula Salad

Preparation Time: 20 minutes
Cooking Time: 0 minutes
Servings: 6

Ingredients:

¼ Cup Olive Oil
6 Cups Kale, Chopped Rough
2 Cups arugula
½ Teaspoon Smoked Paprika
2 Tablespoons Lemon Juice, Fresh
1/3 Cup Pistachios, Unsalted & Shelled
6 Tablespoons Parmesan, Grated

Directions:

1.Get out a large bowl and combine your oil, lemon juice, kale and smoked paprika.

2.Massage it into the leaves for about fifteen seconds. You then need to allow it to sit for ten minutes.

3.Mix everything together before serving with grated cheese on top.

Potato Salad

Preparation Time: 10 minutes
Cooking Time: 15 minutes
Servings: 6

Ingredients:

2 lbs. Golden Potatoes, Cubed in 1 Inch Pieces
3 Tablespoons Olive Oil
3 tablespoons Lemon Juice, Fresh
1 Tablespoon Olive Brine
¼ Teaspoon Sea Salt, Fine
½ Cup Olives, Sliced
1 Cup Celery, Sliced
2 Tablespoons Oregano, Fresh
2 Tablespoons Mint Leaves, Fresh & Chopped

Directions:

1.Get out a medium saucepan and put your potatoes in cold water. The water should be earn inch above your potatoes.

2.Set it over high heat and bring it to a boil before turning the heat down. You want to turn it down to medium-low.

3.Allow it to cook for twelve to fifteen more minutes. The potatoes should be tender when you pierce them with a fork.

4.Get out a small bowl and whisk your oil, lemon juice, olive brine and salt together.

5.Drain your potatoes using a colander and transfer it to a serving bowl. Pour in three tablespoons of dressing over your potatoes, and mix well with oregano, and min along with the remaining dressing.

Raisin Rice Pilaf

Preparation Time: 7 minutes
Cooking Time: 8 minutes
Servings: 5

Ingredients:

1 Tablespoon Olive Oil
1 Teaspoon Cumin
1 Cup Onion, Chopped
½ Cup Carrot, Shredded
½ Teaspoon Cinnamon
2 Cups Instant Brown Rice
1 ¾ Cup Orange Juice
1 Cup Golden Raisins
¼ Cup Water
½ Cup Pistachios, Shelled
Fresh Chives, Chopped for Garnish

Directions:

1.Place a medium saucepan over medium-high heat before adding in your oil.

2.Add n your onion, and stir often so it doesn't burn.

3.Cook for about five minutes and then add in your cumin, cinnamon and carrot. Cook for about another minute.

4.Add in your orange juice, water and rice. Bring it all to a boil before covering your saucepan.

5.Turn the heat down to medium-low and then allow it to simmer for six to seven minutes. Your rice should be cooked all the way through, and all the liquid should be absorbed.

6.Stir in your pistachios, chives and raisins. Serve warm.

Lebanesen Delight

Preparation Time: 10 minutes
Cooking Time: 15 minutes
Servings: 5

Ingredients:

1 Tablespoon Olive Oil
1 Cup Vermicelli (Can be Substituted for Thin Spaghetti)
Broken into 1 to 1
½ inch Pieces
3 Cups Cabbage, Shredded
3 Cups Vegetable Broth, Low Sodium
½ Cup Water
1 Cup Instant Brown Rice
¼ Teaspoon Sea Salt, Fine
2 Cloves Garlic
¼ Teaspoon Crushed Red Pepper
½ Cup Cilantro Fresh & Chopped Lemon Slices to
Garnish

Directions:

1.Get out a saucepan and then place it over medium-high heat.

2.Add in your oil and once it's hot you will need to add in your pasta.

3.Cook for three minutes or until your pasta is toasted. You will have to stir often in order to keep it from burning.

4.Add in your cabbage, cooking for another four minutes. Continue to stir often.

5.Add in your water and rice. Season with salt, red pepper and garlic before bringing it all to a boil over high heat. Stir, and then cover.

6.Once it's covered turn the heat down to medium-low. Allow it all to simmer for ten minutes.

7.Remove the pan from the burner and then allow it to sit without lifting the lid for five minutes. Take the garlic cloves out and then mash them using a fork.

8.Place them back in, and stir them into the rice. Stir in your cilantro as well and serve warm. Garnish with lemon wedges if desired.

Mediterranean Sweet Potato

Preparation Time: 10 minutes
Cooking Time: 25 minutes
Servings: 4

Ingredients:

4 Sweet Potatoes
15 Ounce Can Chickpeas, Rinsed & Drained
½ Tablespoon Olive Oil
½ Teaspoon Cumin
½ Teaspoon Coriander
½ Teaspoon Cinnamon
1 Pinch Sea Salt, Fine
½ Teaspoon Paprika
¼ Cup Hummus
1 Tablespoon Lemon Juice, Fresh 2-3 Teaspoon Dill, Fresh
3 Cloves Garlic, Minced
Unsweetened Almond Milk as Needed

Directions:

1.Start by preheating your oven to 400, and then get out a baking sheet. Line it with foil.

2.Wash your sweet potatoes before halving them lengthwise.

3.Take your olive oil, cumin, chickpeas, coriander, sea salt and paprika on your baking sheet. Rub the sweet potatoes with olive oil, placing them face down over the mixture.

4.Roast for twenty to twenty-five minutes. They should become tender, and your chickpeas should turn a golden color.

5.Once it's in the oven, you can prepare your sauce. To do this mix your dill, lemon juice, hummus, garlic and a dash of almond milk. Mix well. Add more almond milk to thin as necessary. Adjust the seasoning if necessary.

6.Smash the insides of the sweet potato down, topping with chickpea mixture and sauce before serving.

Flavorful Braised Kale

Preparation Time: 15 minutes
Cooking Time: 15 minutes
Servings: 6

Ingredients:

1 lb. Kale, Stems Removed & Chopped Roughly
1 Cup Cherry Tomatoes, Halved
2 Teaspoons Olive Oil
4 Cloves Garlic, Sliced Thin
½ Cup Vegetable Stock
¼ Teaspoon Sea Salt, Fine
1 Tablespoon Lemon Juice, Fresh
1/8 Teaspoon Black Pepper

Directions:

1.Start by heating your olive oil in a frying pan using medium heat, and add in your garlic. Sauté for a minute or two until lightly golden.

2.Mix your kale and vegetable stock with your garlic, adding it to your pan. Cover the pan and then turn the heat down to medium-low.

3.Allow it to cook until your kale wilts and part of your vegetable stock should be dissolved. It should take roughly five minutes.

4.Stir in your tomatoes and cook without a lid until your kale is tender, and then remove it from heat.

5.Mix in your salt, pepper and lemon juice before serving warm.

Bean Salad

Preparation Time: 15 minutes
Cooking Time: 5 minutes
Servings: 6

Ingredients:

1 Can Garbanzo Beans, Rinsed & Drained
2 Tablespoons Balsamic Vinegar
¼ Cup Olive Oil
4 Cloves Garlic, Chopped Fine
1/3 Cup Parsley, Fresh & Chopped
¼ Cup Olive Oil
1 Red Onion, Diced 6 Lettuce Leaves
½ Cup Celery, Chopped Fine/Black Pepper to Taste

Directions:

1.Make the vinaigrette dressing by whipping together your garlic, parsley, vinegar and pepper in a bowl.

2.Add the olive oil to this mixture and whisk before setting it aside.

3.Add in your onion and beans, and then pour your dressing on top. Toss until it's coated together and then cover it. Place it in the fridge until it's time to serve.

4.Place a lettuce leaf on the plate when serving and spoon the mixture in. garnish with celery.

Basil Tomato Skewers

Preparation Time: 10 minutes
Cooking Time: 0 minutes
Servings: 2

Ingredients:

16 Mozzarella Balls, Fresh & Small
16 Basil Leaves, Fresh
16 Cherry Tomatoes Olive Oil to Drizzle
Sea Salt & Black Pepper to Taste

Directions:

1.Start by threading your basil, cheese and tomatoes together on small skewers.

2.Drizzle with oil before seasoning with salt and pepper.

3.Serve immediately.

Olives with Feta

Preparation Time: 5 minutes
Cooking Time: 0 minutes
Servings: 4

Ingredients:

½ Cup Feta Cheese, Diced
1 Cup Kalamata Olives, Sliced & Pitted
2 Cloves Garlic, Sliced
2 Tablespoons Olive Oil
1 Lemon, Zested & Juiced
1 Teaspoon Rosemary, Fresh & Chopped Crushed Red
Pepper
Black Pepper to Taste

Directions:

1.Mix everything together and serve over crackers.

Black Bean Medley

Preparation Time: 5 minutes
Cooking Time: 0 minutes
Servings: 4

Ingredients:

4 Plum Tomatoes, Chopped
14.5 Ounces Black Beans, Canned & Drained
½ Red Onion, Sliced
¼ Cup Dill, Fresh & Chopped
1 Lemon, Juiced
2 Tablespoons Olive Oil
¼ Cup Feta Cheese, Crumbled
Sea Salt to Taste

Directions:

1.Mix everything in a bowl except for your feta and salt.
Top the beans with salt and feta.

Spiced Popcorn

Preparation Time: 5 minutes
Cooking Time: 5 minutes
Servings: 4

Ingredients:

3 tablespoons olive oil
½ cup popcorn kernels Cooking spray
1 teaspoon garlic powder
1 teaspoon onion powder
½ teaspoon smoked paprika
½ teaspoon salt
⅛ Teaspoon cayenne pepper

Directions:

1.In a medium pot over medium-low heat, heat the olive oil.

2.Add 3 popcorn kernels, and when one of the kernels pops, add the rest.

3.Cover and shake the pot occasionally to prevent burning. Once fully popped, transfer the popcorn to a large bowl.

4.Spray the popcorn with cooking spray. Use clean hands to toss the popcorn, mixing it thoroughly.

5.In a small bowl, mix together the garlic powder, onion powder, paprika, salt, and cayenne.

6.Sprinkle the spice mix over the popcorn, and toss until the popcorn is thoroughly coated.

Baked Spinach Chips

Preparation Time: 5 minutes
Cooking Time: 15 minutes
Servings: 4

Ingredients:

Cooking spray
5 ounces baby spinach, washed and patted dry
2 tablespoons olive oil
1 teaspoon garlic powder
½ teaspoon salt
⅛ Teaspoon freshly ground black pepper

Directions:

1.Preheat the oven to 350°F. Coat two baking sheets with cooking spray.

2.Place the spinach in a large bowl. Add the olive oil, garlic powder, salt, and pepper, and toss until evenly coated.

3.Spread the spinach in a single layer on the baking sheets. Bake for 12 to 15 minutes, until the spinach leaves are crisp and slightly browned.

4.Store spinach chips in a resalable container at room temperature for up to 1 week.

Peanut Butter Yogurt Dip with Fruit

Preparation Time: 10 minutes
Cooking Time: 0 minutes
Servings: 4

Ingredients:

1cup nonfat vanilla Greek yogurt
2tablespoons natural creamy peanut butter
2teaspoons honey
1pear, cored and sliced
1 apple, cored and sliced
1 banana, sliced

Directions:

1.In a medium bowl, whisk together the yogurt, peanut butter, and honey.

2.Serve the dip with the fruit on the side.

Snickerdoodle Pecans

Preparation Time: 10 minutes
Cooking Time: 15 minutes
Servings: 8

Ingredients:

Cooking spray
1½ cups raw pecans
2 tablespoons brown sugar
2 tablespoons 100% maple syrup
½ teaspoon ground cinnamon
½ teaspoon vanilla extract
⅛ Teaspoon salt

Directions:

1.Preheat the oven to 350°F. Line a baking sheet with parchment paper and coat with cooking spray.

2.In a medium bowl, place the pecans. Add the brown sugar, maple syrup, cinnamon, vanilla, and salt, tossing to evenly coat.

3.Spread the pecans in a single layer on the prepared baking sheet. Bake for about 12 minutes, until pecans are slightly browned and fragrant.

4.Remove and set aside to cool for 10 minutes.

Almond-Stuffed Dates

Preparation Time: 5 minutes
Cooking Time: 0 minutes
Servings: 4

Ingredients:

20 raw almonds
20 pitted dates

Directions:

1.Place one almond into each of 20 dates.

2.Serve at room temperature.

Peanut Butter Chocolate Chip Energy Bites

Preparation Time: 20 minutes
Cooking Time: 5 minutes
Servings: 12

Ingredients:

1 cup gluten-free old-fashioned oats
¾ cup natural creamy peanut butter
½ cup unsweetened coconut flakes
½ teaspoon vanilla extract
2 tablespoons honey
¼ cup dark chocolate chips

Directions:

1.Preheat the oven to 350°F. Line a baking sheet with parchment paper.

2.Spread the oats on the prepared baking sheet. Bake for 5 minutes, until the oats are browned. Remove from the oven, and set aside to cool for 5 minutes.

3.In a food processor or blender, add the oats, peanut butter, coconut, vanilla, and honey. Blend until smooth.

3.Transfer the batter into a medium bowl, and fold in the chocolate chips. Spoon out a tablespoon of batter.

4.Use clean hands to roll into a 2-inch ball, and place on the baking sheet. Repeat for the remaining batter, making a total of 12 balls.

5.Place the baking sheet in the refrigerator to allow the bites to set, at least 15 minutes.

No-Cook Pistachio-Cranberry Quinoa Bites

Preparation Time: 15 minutes
Cooking Time: 0 minutes
Servings: 12

Ingredients:

½ cup quinoa
¾ cup natural almond butter
¾ cup gluten-free old-fashioned oats
2 tablespoons honey
⅛ Teaspoon salt
¼ cup unsalted shelled pistachios, roughly chopped
¼ cup dried cranberries

Directions:

1. In a blender, add the quinoa and blend until it turns into a flour consistency. Add the almond butter, oats, honey, and salt, and blend until smooth.

2. Transfer the mixture into a medium bowl, and gently fold in the pistachios and cranberries.

3. Spoon out a tablespoon of the batter. Use clean hands to roll into a 2-inch ball, and place into a container.
4. Repeat for the remaining batter, making a total of 12 balls.

5. Place the container in the refrigerator to allow the bites to set, at least 15 minutes.

No-Bake Honey-Almond Granola Bars

Preparation Time: 15 minutes
Cooking Time: 0 minutes
Servings: 8

Ingredients:

Cooking spray
1 cup pitted dates
¼ cup honey
¾ cup natural creamy almond butter
¾ cup gluten-free rolled oats
2 tablespoons raw almonds, chopped
2 tablespoons pumpkin seeds

Directions:

1.Line an 8-by-8-inch baking dish with parchment paper, and coat the paper with cooking spray.

2.In a food processor or blender, add the dates and blend until they reach a pastelike consistency. Add the honey, almond butter, and oats, and blend until well combined. Transfer the mixture to a medium bowl.

3.Add the almonds and pumpkin seeds, and gently fold until well combined. Spoon the mixture into the prepared baking dish. Spread the mixture evenly, using clean fingers to push down the mixture so it is compact.

4.Cover with plastic wrap and refrigerate until the bars set, 1 to 2 hours. Remove from the refrigerator and cut into 8 bars.

5.Carefully remove each bar from the baking dish, and wrap individually in plastic wrap. Place bars in the refrigerator until ready to grab and go.

Cottage Cheese–Filled Avocado

Preparation Time: 5 minutes
Cooking Time: 0 minutes
Servings: 4

Ingredients:

½ cup low-fat cottage cheese
¼ cup cherry tomatoes, quartered
2 avocados, halved and pitted
4 teaspoons pumpkin seeds
¼ teaspoon salt
⅛ Teaspoon freshly ground black pepper

Directions:

1.In a small bowl, mix together the cottage cheese and tomatoes.

2.Spoon 2 tablespoons of the cheese-tomato mixture onto each of the avocado halves.

3.Top each with 1 teaspoon of pumpkin seeds, and sprinkle with the salt and pepper.

Avocado Toast with Balsamic Glaze

Preparation Time: 5 minutes
Cooking Time: 10 minutes
Servings: 2

Ingredients:

¼ cup balsamic vinegar
1 tablespoon brown sugar
1 ripe avocado, halved and pitted
2 slices 100% whole-wheat bread, toasted
5 cherry tomatoes, halved
⅛ Teaspoon salt
⅛ Teaspoon freshly ground black pepper

Directions:

1.In a small saucepan over medium heat, heat the vinegar and brown sugar, stirring constantly, until the sugar dissolves.

2.Bring the mixture to a boil, lower heat, and simmer for about 10 minutes, until the vinegar is reduced by half and thickens.

3.Set aside to cool for 10 minutes.
Scoop out the flesh from each avocado half onto a slice of toasted bread.

4.Mash the avocado with a fork until it is flattened.

5.Top each slice of bread with 5 tomato halves, and sprinkle with the salt and pepper.

6.Drizzle about ½ tablespoon of the balsamic glaze on each avocado toast.

CPSIA information can be obtained
at www.ICGtesting.com
Printed in the USA
BVHW061746230421
605732BV00006B/898